NARWHAL
UNICORN OF THE SEA

BEN CLANTON

TUNDRA BOOKS

FOR ENYA
A.K.A. NUNU, A.K.A. JELLYFISH-FLINGER,
A.K.A. MERMICORN

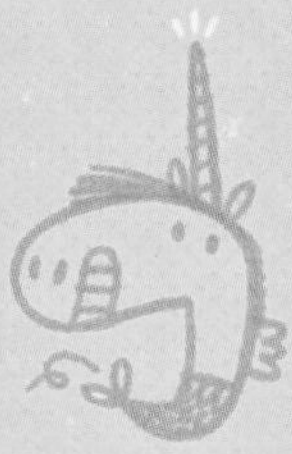

Tundra Books, a division of Random House of Canada Limited, a Penguin Random House Company

Library and Archives Canada Cataloguing in Publication

Clanton, Ben, 1988-, author, illustrator
Narwhal : unicorn of the sea / written and illustrated
by Ben Clanton.

Issued in print and electronic formats.
ISBN 978-1-101-91826-5 (bound).–ISBN 978-1-101-91871-5 (paperback)
ISBN 978-1-101-91827-2 (epub)

I. Title.

PZ7.C523Na 2016 j813'.6 C2015-905757-4
C2015-905758-2

Published simultaneously in the United States of America by Tundra Books of Northern New York, a division of Random House of Canada Limited, a Penguin Random House Company

Library of Congress Control Number: 2015955122

Edited by Tara Walker
Designed by Ben Clanton and Andrew Roberts
The artwork in this book was rendered in colored pencil and colored digitally.
The text was hand-lettered by Ben Clanton.
Photos: (waffle) © Tiger Images/Shutterstock; (strawberry) © Valentina Razumova/Shutterstock
Printed and bound in the USA

www.penguinrandomhouse.ca

3 4 5 20 19 18 17 16

TUNDRA BOOKS | Penguin Random House

CONTENTS

5 NARWHAL IS REALLY AWESOME

21 REALLY FUN FACTS

23 NARWHAL'S POD OF AWESOMENESS

41 THE NARWHAL SONG

43 NARWHAL AND THE BEST BOOK EVER

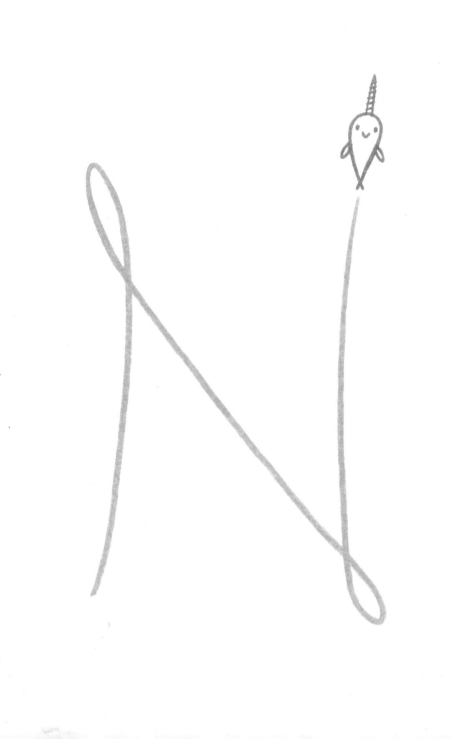

NARWHAL IS REAL_ly AWESOME

ONE DAY WHEN NARWHAL WAS OUT FOR A SWIM, HE FOUND HIMSELF IN NEW WATERS.

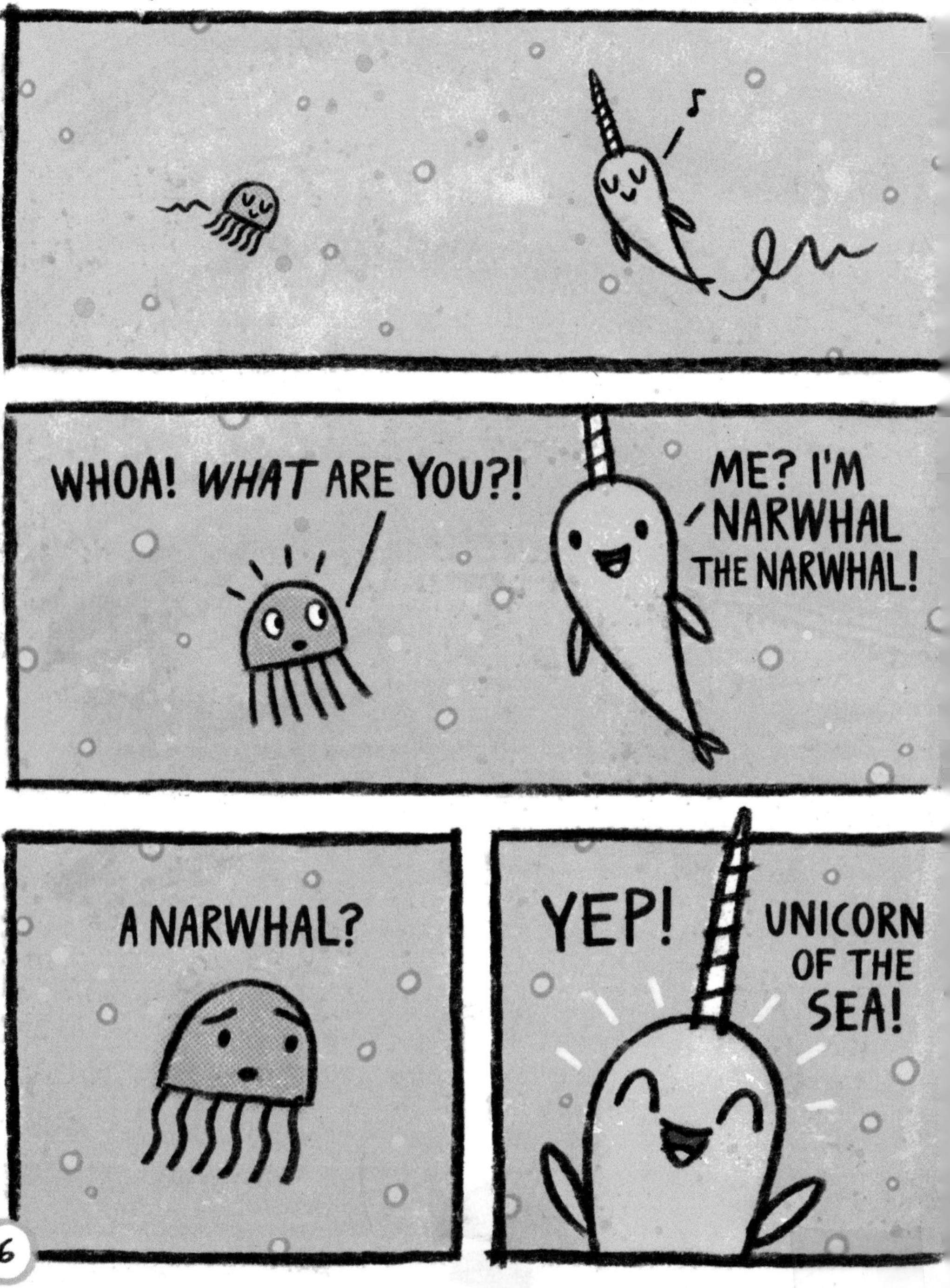
WHOA! *WHAT* ARE YOU?!
ME? I'M NARWHAL THE NARWHAL!
A NARWHAL?
YEP!
UNICORN OF THE SEA!

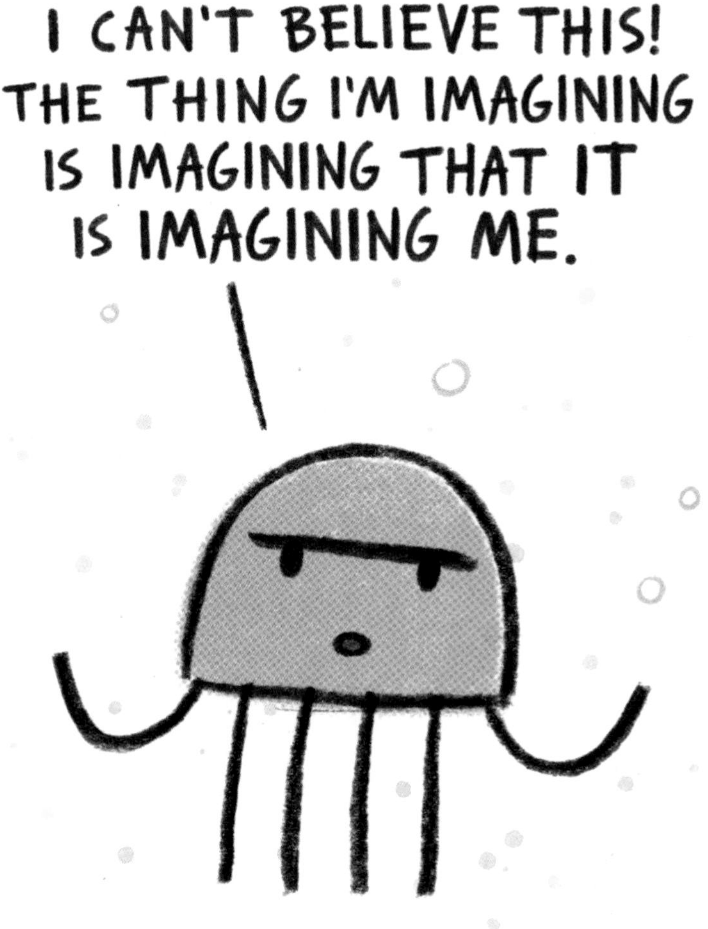
I CAN'T BELIEVE THIS! THE THING I'M IMAGINING IS IMAGINING THAT IT IS IMAGINING ME.

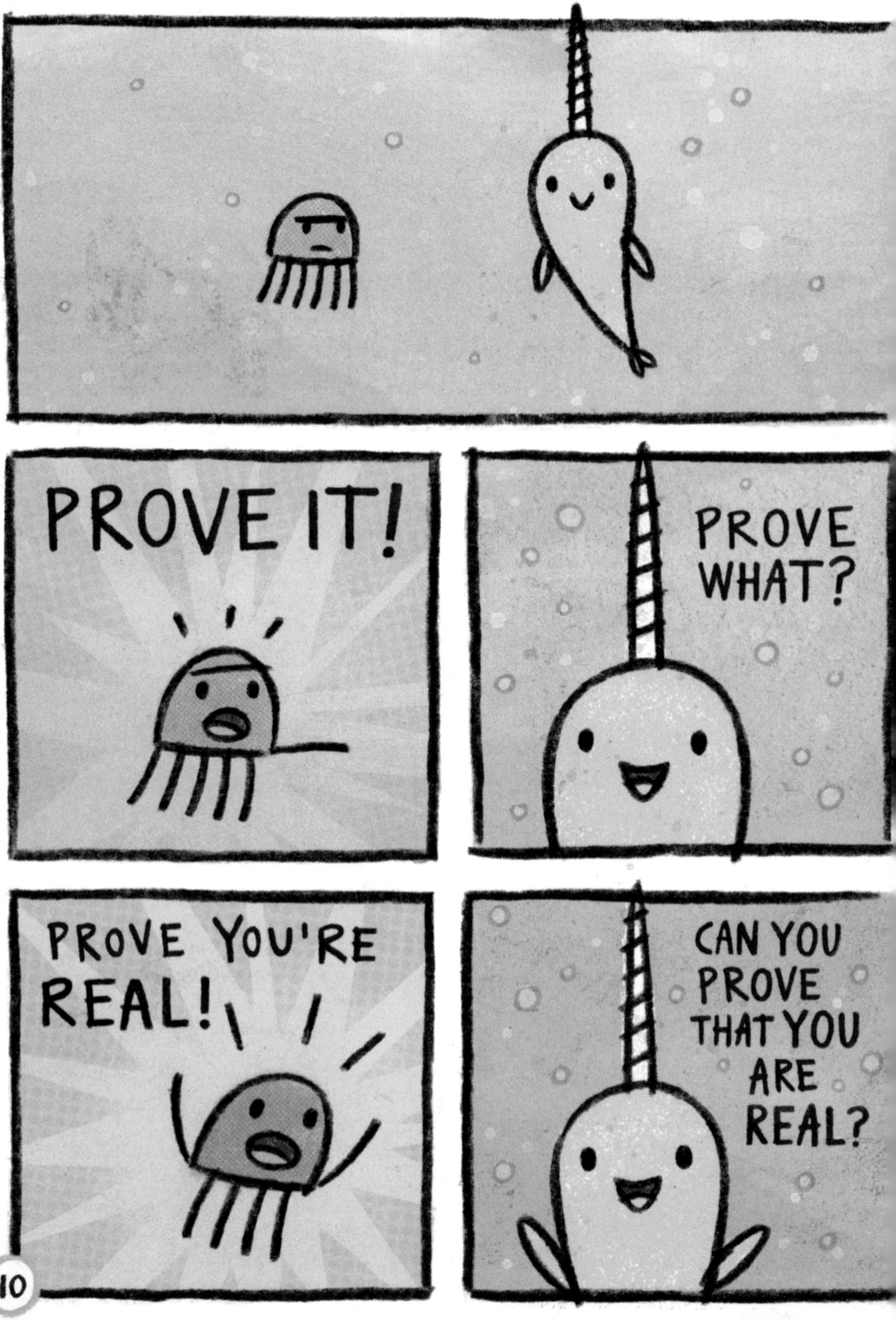
PROVE IT!
PROVE WHAT?
PROVE YOU'RE REAL!
CAN YOU PROVE THAT YOU ARE REAL?

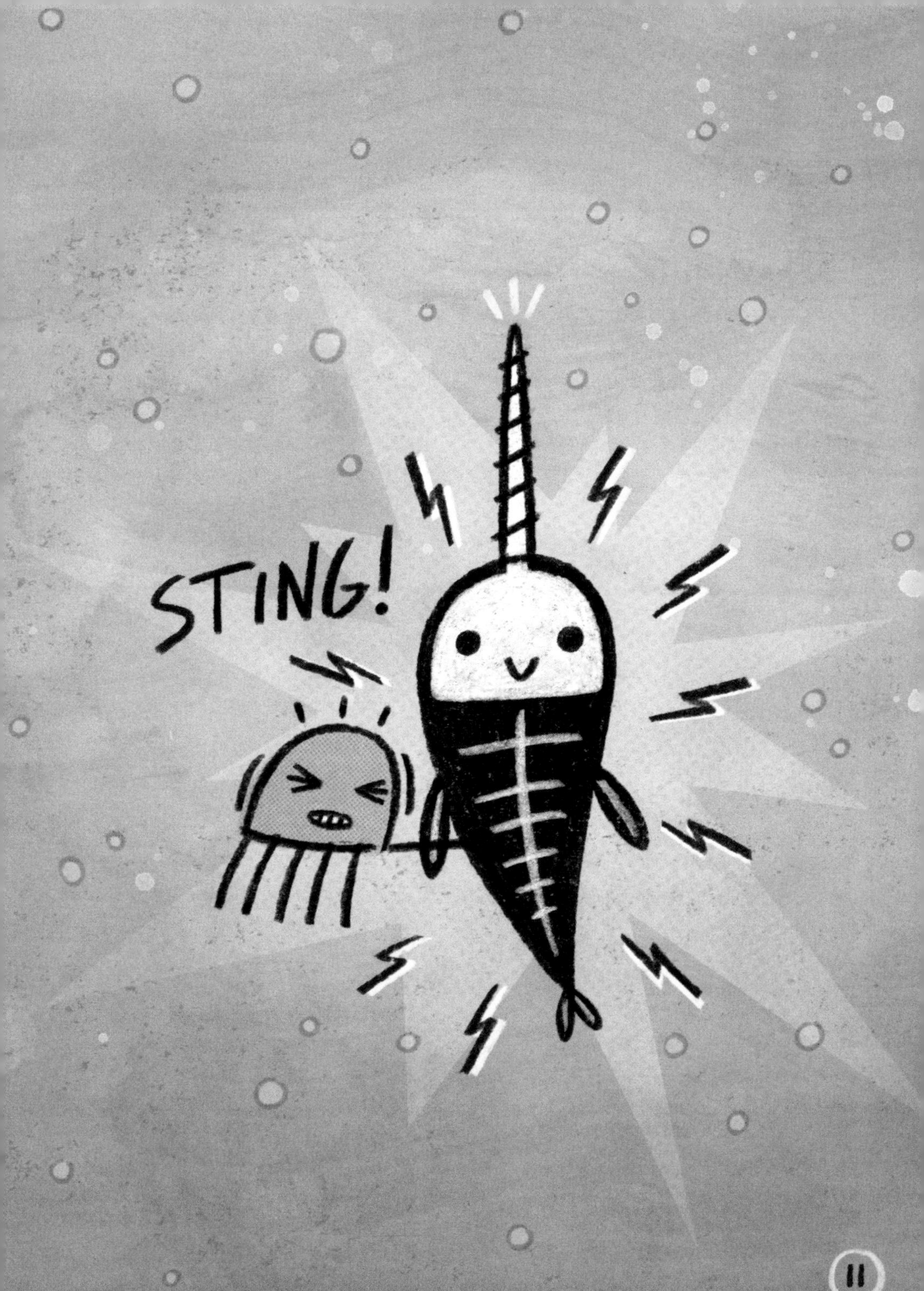
STING!

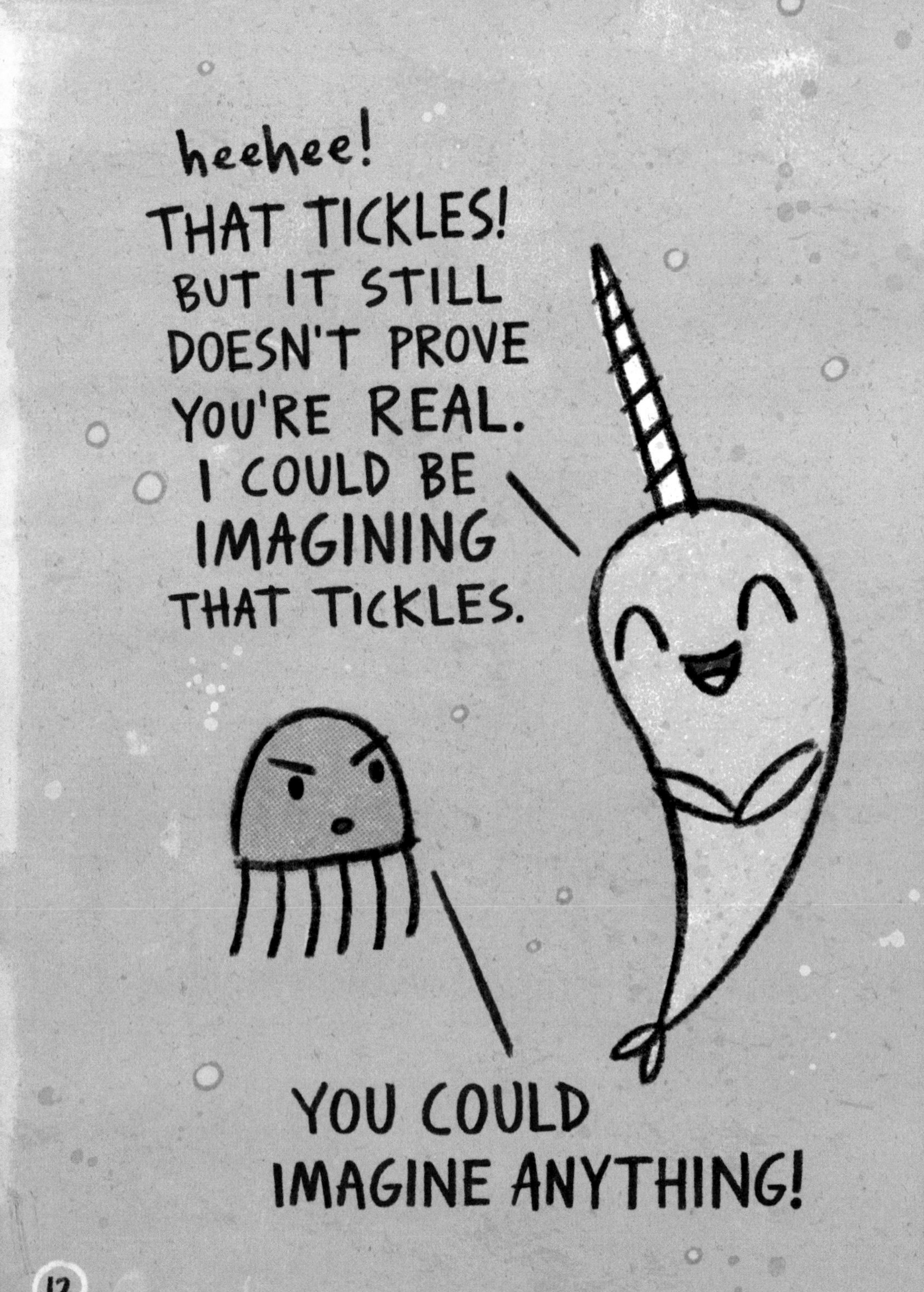

heehee!
THAT TICKLES! BUT IT STILL DOESN'T PROVE YOU'RE REAL. I COULD BE IMAGINING THAT TICKLES.
YOU COULD IMAGINE ANYTHING!

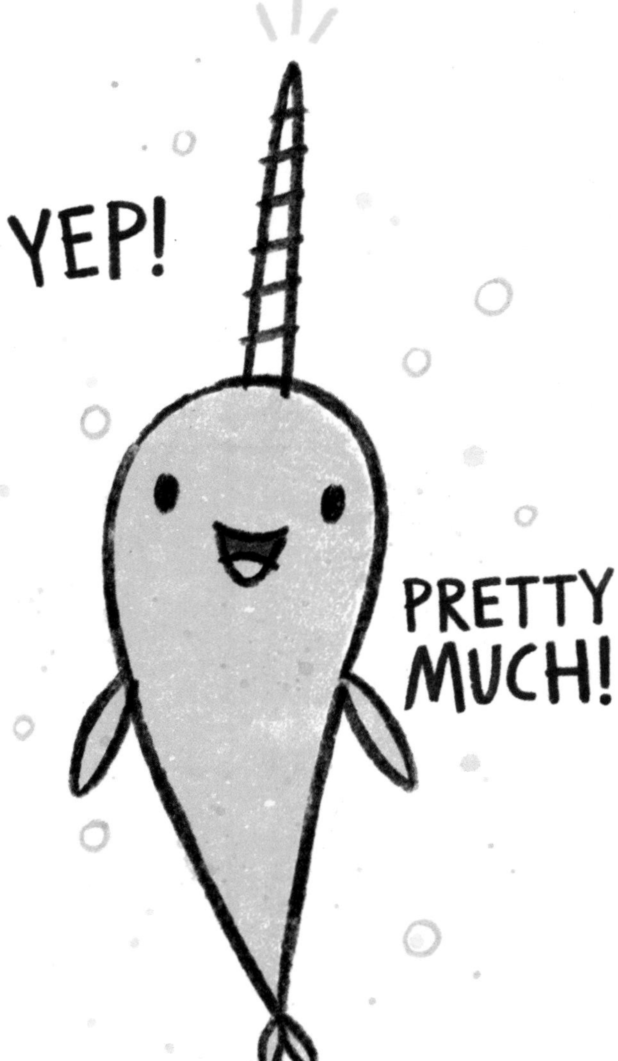
YEP!
PRETTY MUCH!

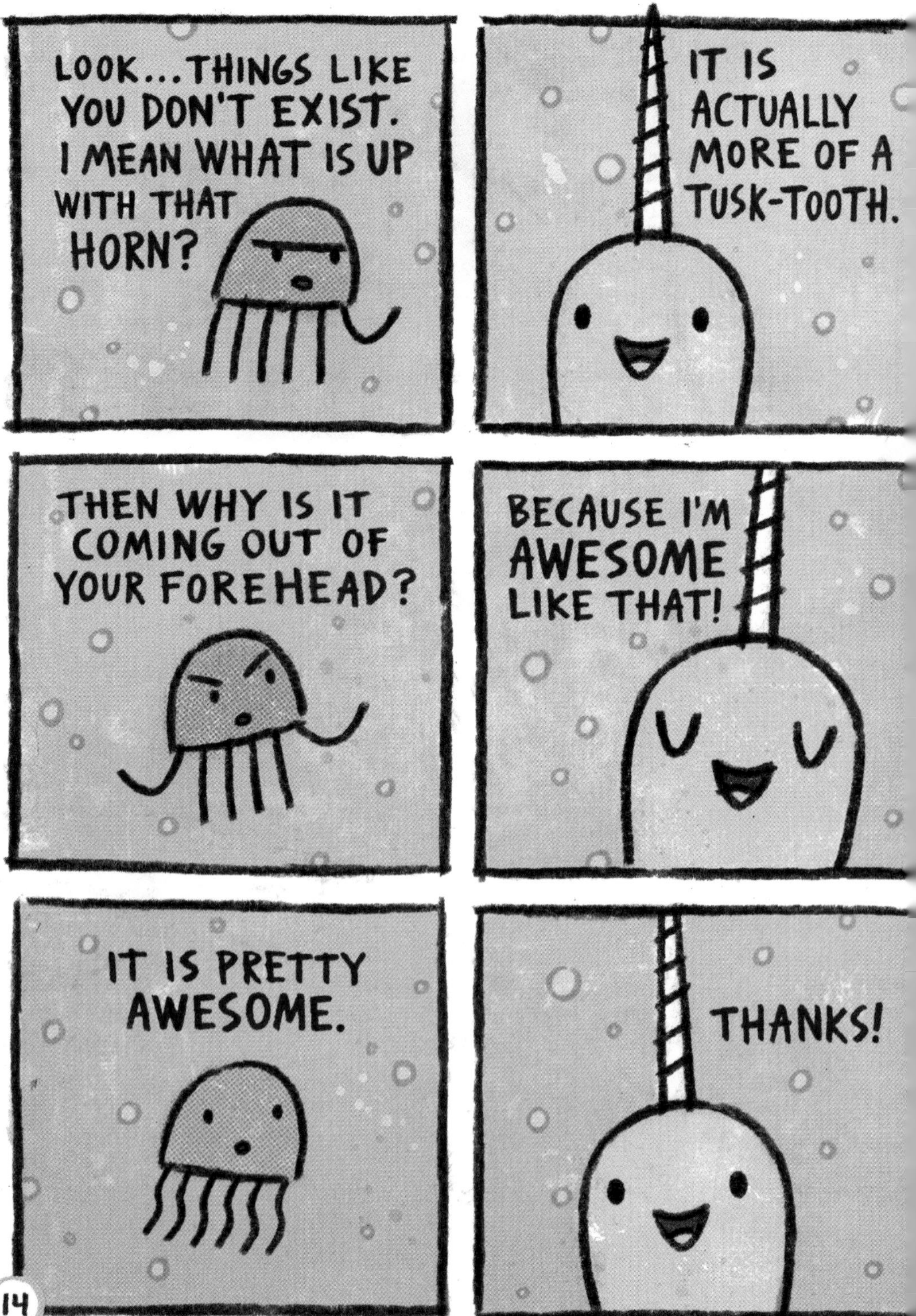
LOOK...THINGS LIKE YOU DON'T EXIST. I MEAN WHAT IS UP WITH THAT HORN?
IT IS ACTUALLY MORE OF A TUSK-TOOTH.
THEN WHY IS IT COMING OUT OF YOUR FOREHEAD?
BECAUSE I'M AWESOME LIKE THAT!
IT IS PRETTY AWESOME.
THANKS!

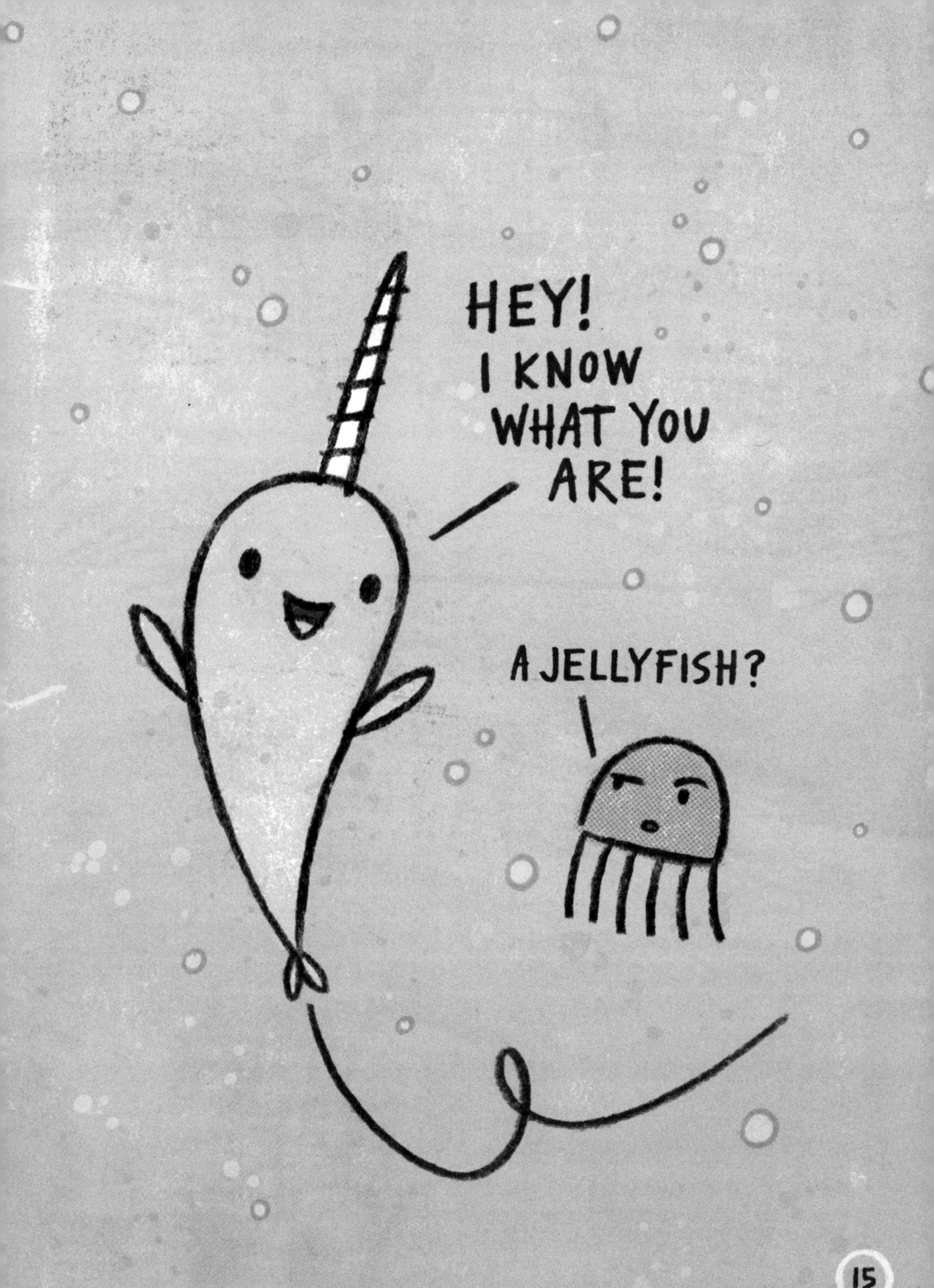
HEY! I KNOW WHAT YOU ARE!
A JELLYFISH?

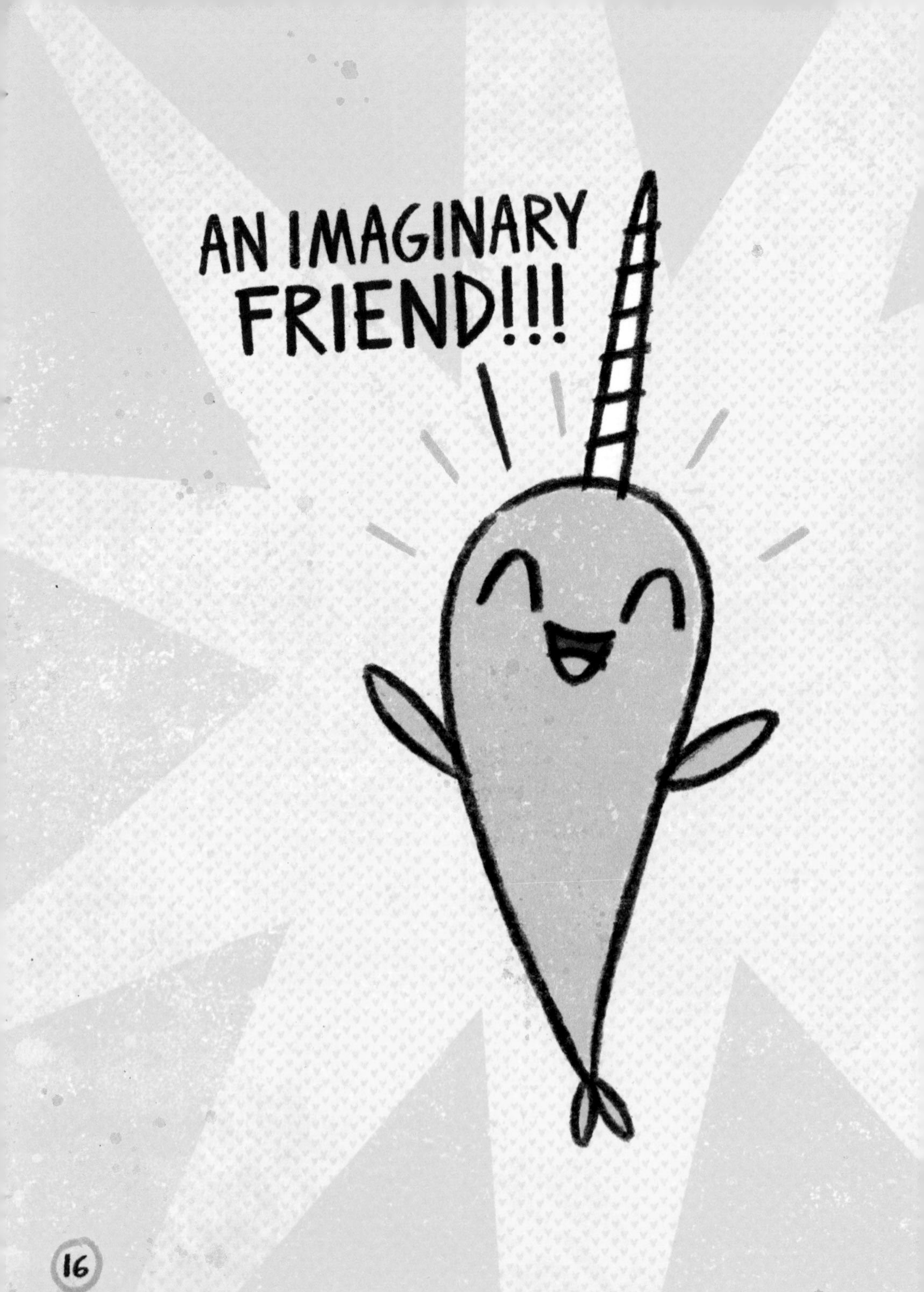
AN IMAGINARY FRIEND!!!

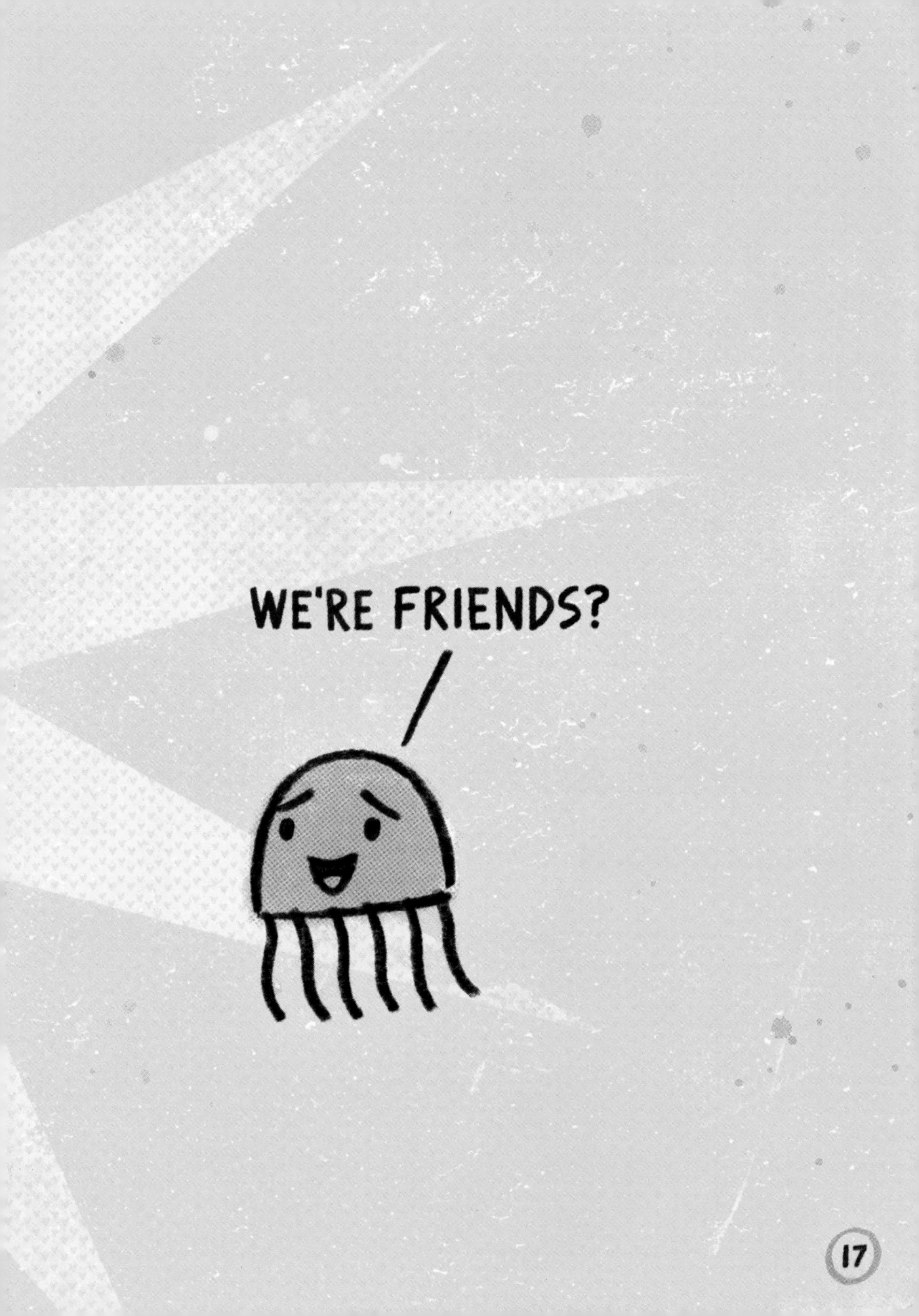
WE'RE FRIENDS?

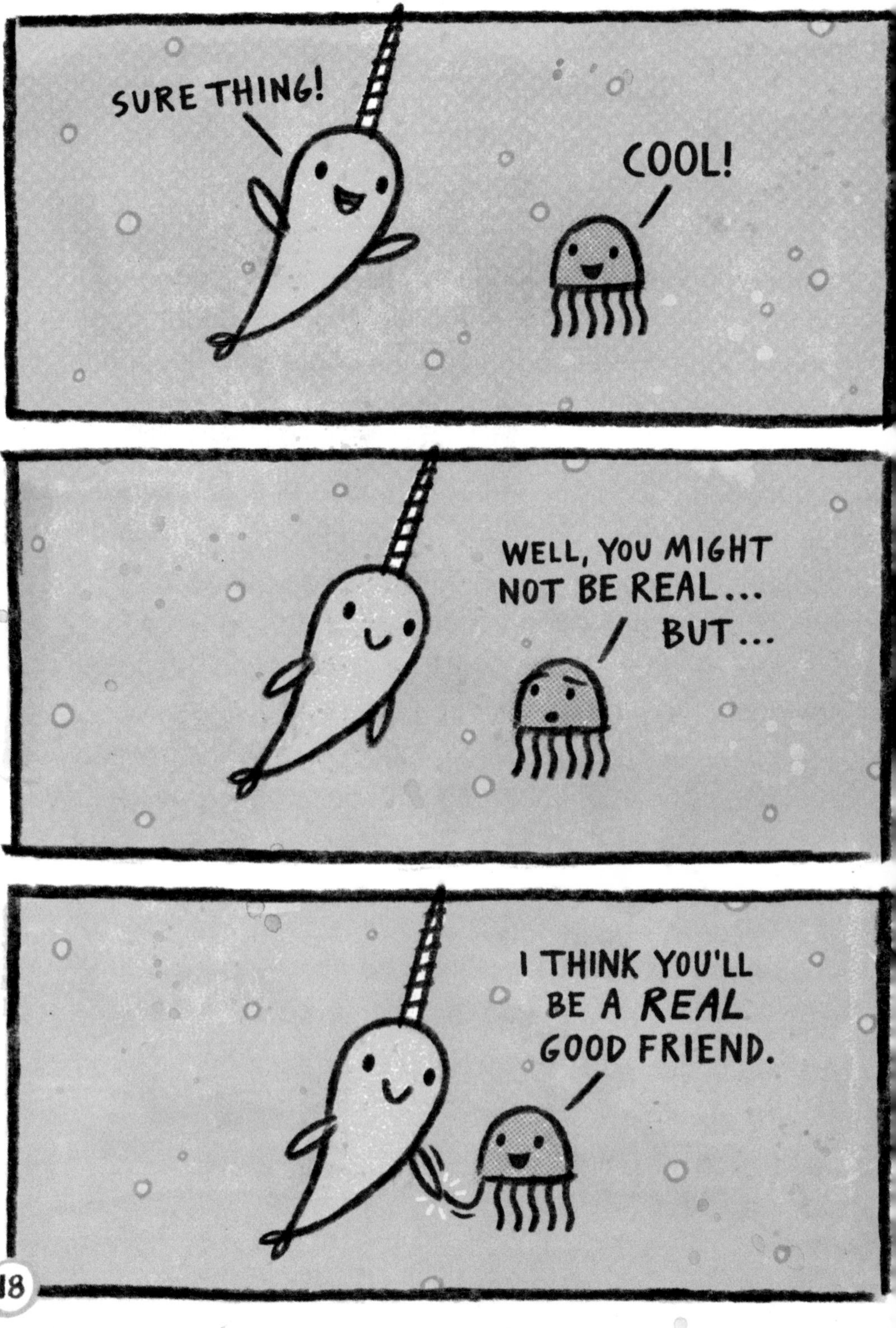
SURE THING!
COOL!
WELL, YOU MIGHT NOT BE REAL... BUT...
I THINK YOU'LL BE A REAL GOOD FRIEND.

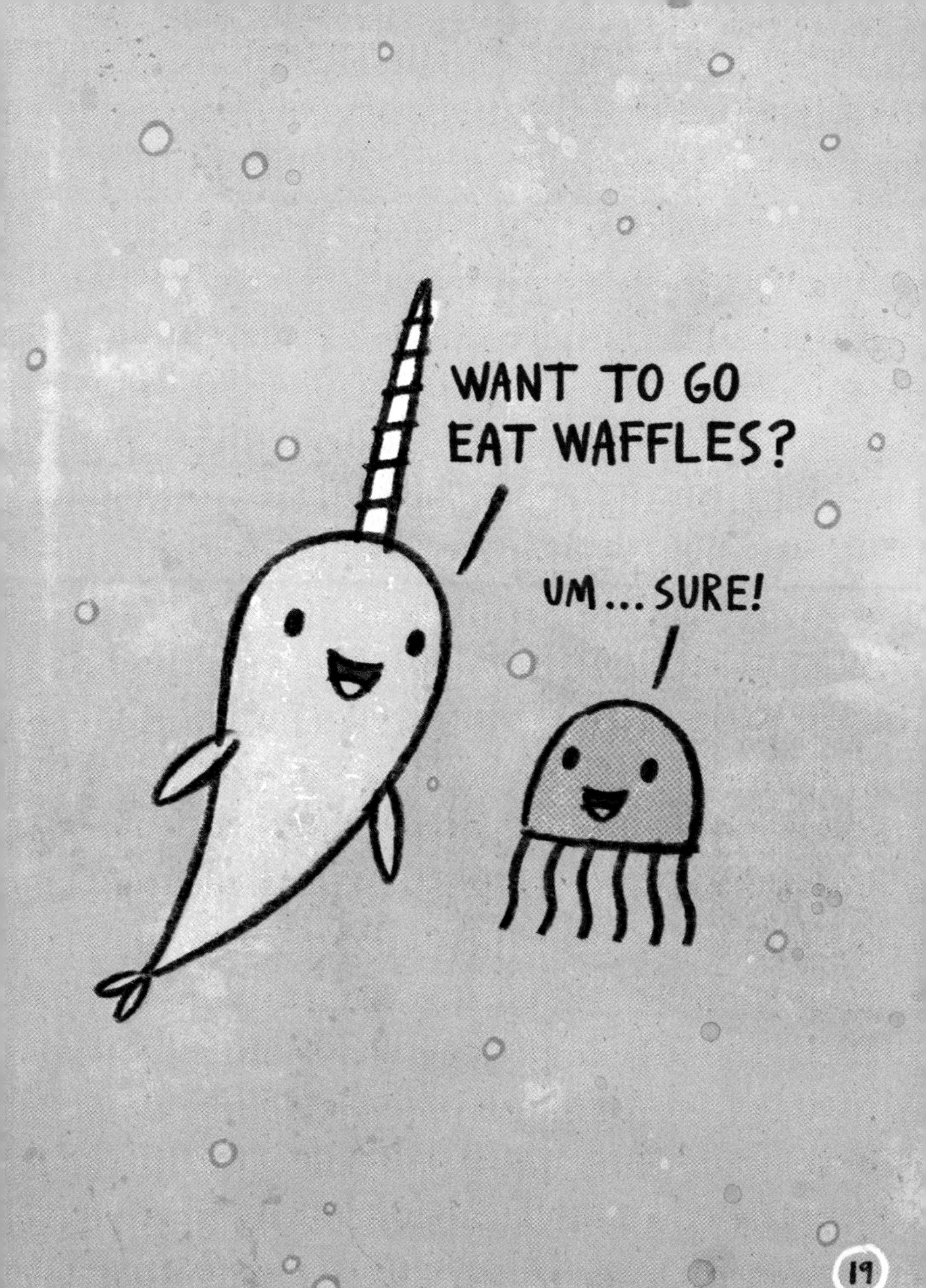
WANT TO GO EAT WAFFLES?
UM... SURE!

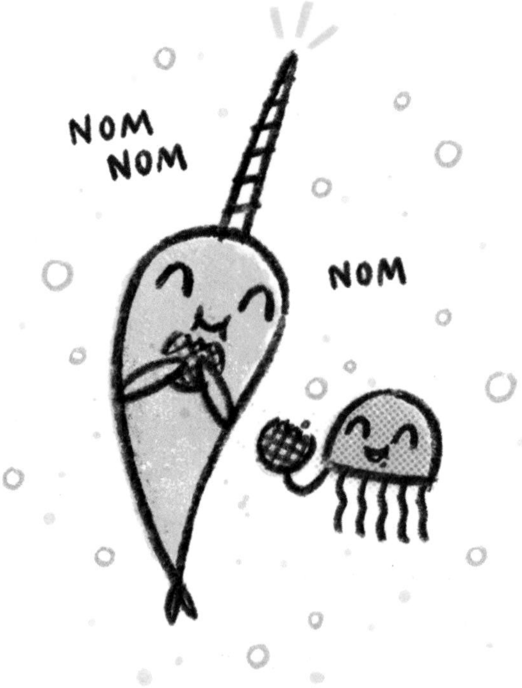
NOM
NOM
NOM

REALLY FUN FACTS

A NARWHAL'S LONG, HORN-LIKE TOOTH CAN REACH UP TO 3 m (10 ft.) LONG!

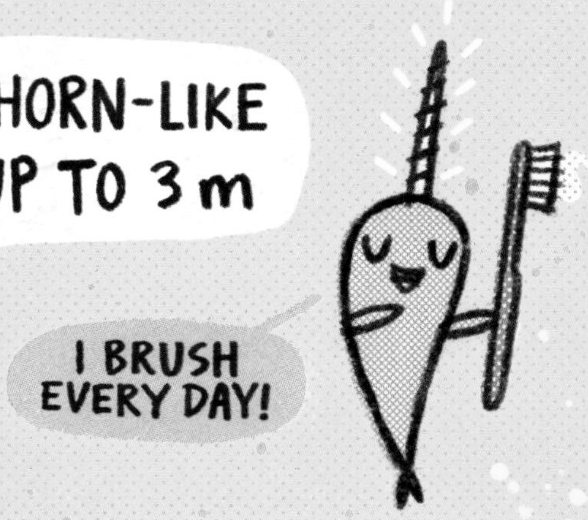
I BRUSH EVERY DAY!

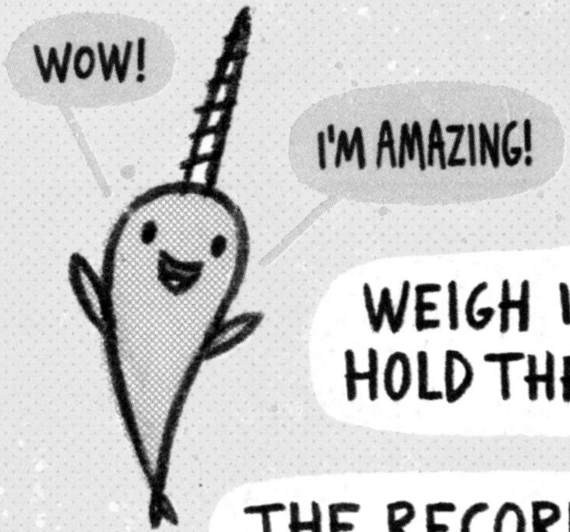
WOW!
I'M AMAZING!

NARWHALS CAN WEIGH 1,600 kg (3,500 lb.) AND HOLD THEIR BREATH FOR 25 min.

THE RECORD DIVE DEPTH FOR A NARWHAL IS 1,800 m (5,905 ft., OVER ONE MILE).

RECENT RESEARCH SUGGESTS NARWHALS CAN LIVE UP TO 90 YEARS.

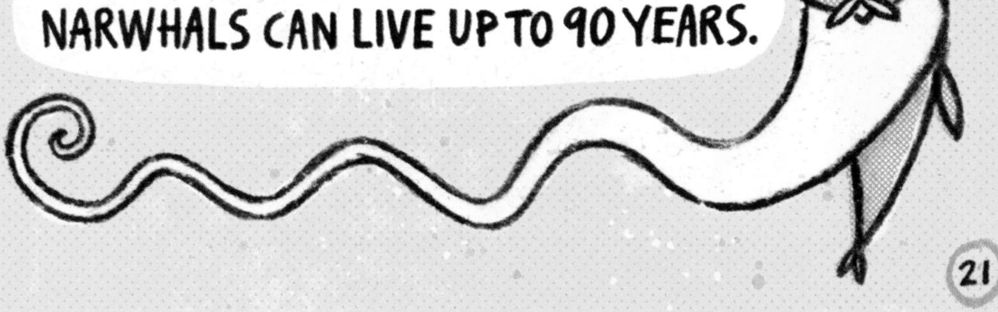

MORE REALLY FUN FACTS

THERE ARE NEARLY 4,000 TYPES OF JELLYFISH IN THE WORLD.

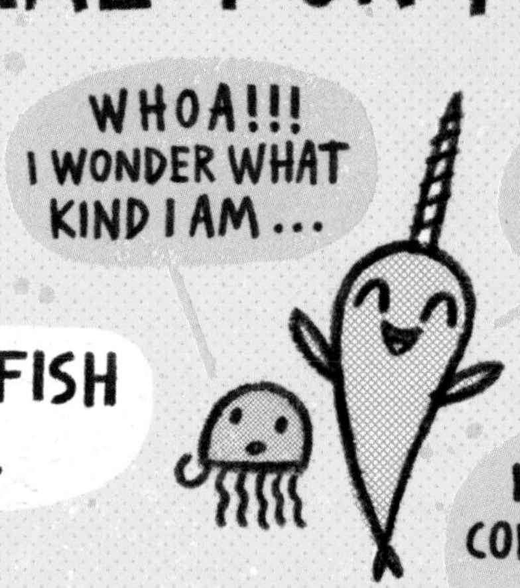
WHOA!!! I WONDER WHAT KIND I AM...
THE AWESOME KIND!

A GROUP OF JELLYFISH IS CALLED A SMACK.

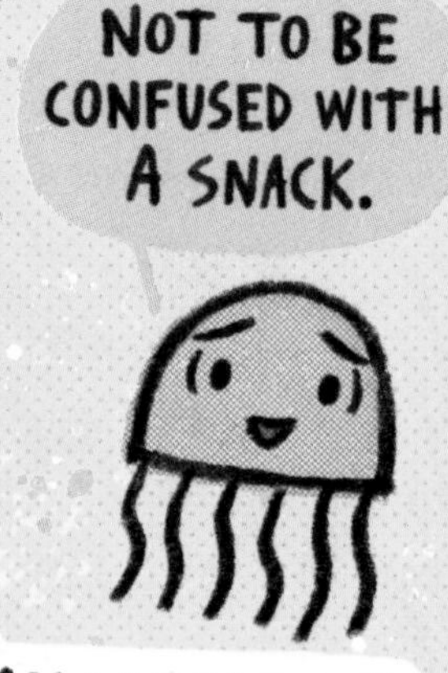
NOT TO BE CONFUSED WITH A SNACK.

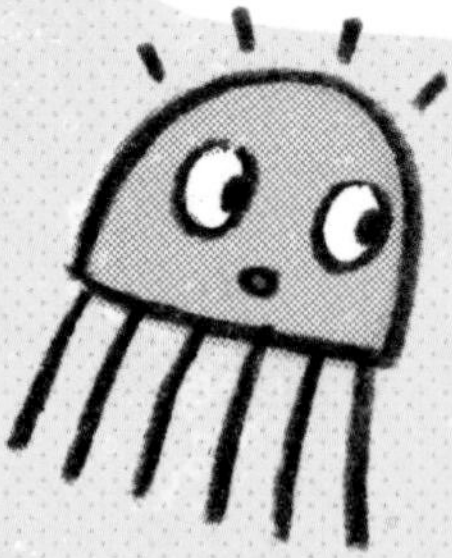

JELLYFISH HAVE BEEN AROUND FOR MILLIONS OF YEARS. WELL BEFORE DINOSAURS!

THE STING FROM SOME JELLYFISH CAN BE DEADLY FOR HUMANS.

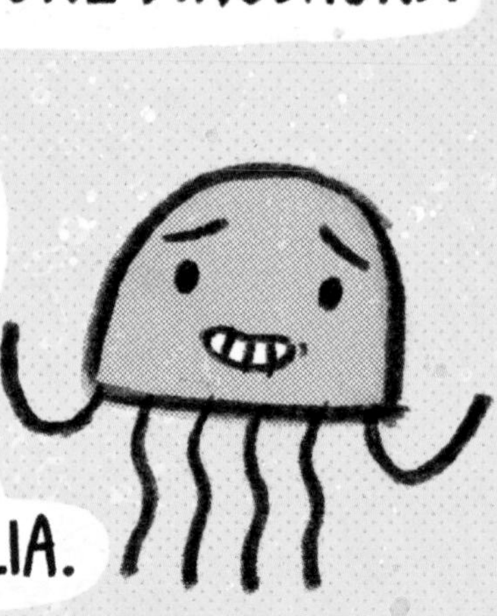

THE DEADLY ONES ARE FOUND MAINLY IN AUSTRALIA.

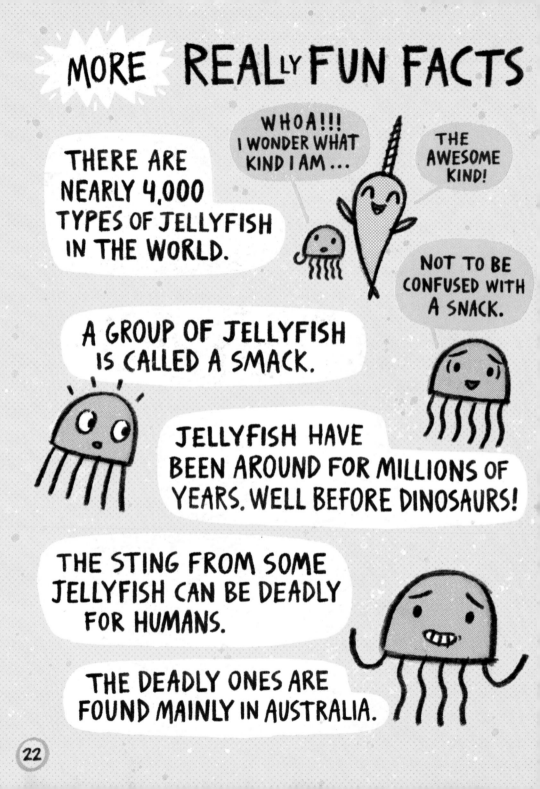

NARWHAL'S POD OF AWESOMENESS

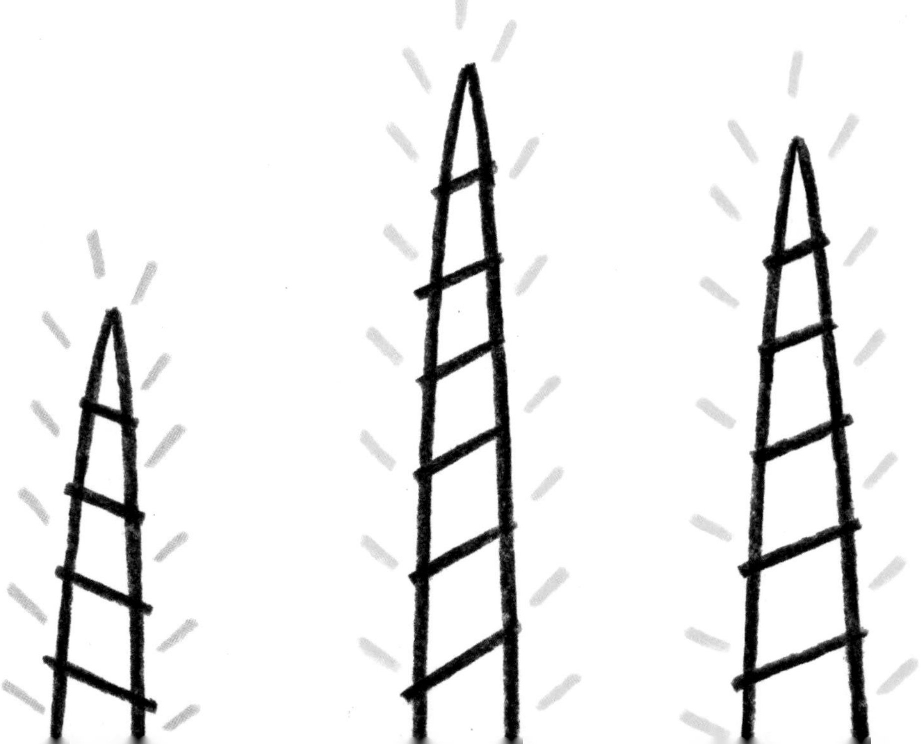

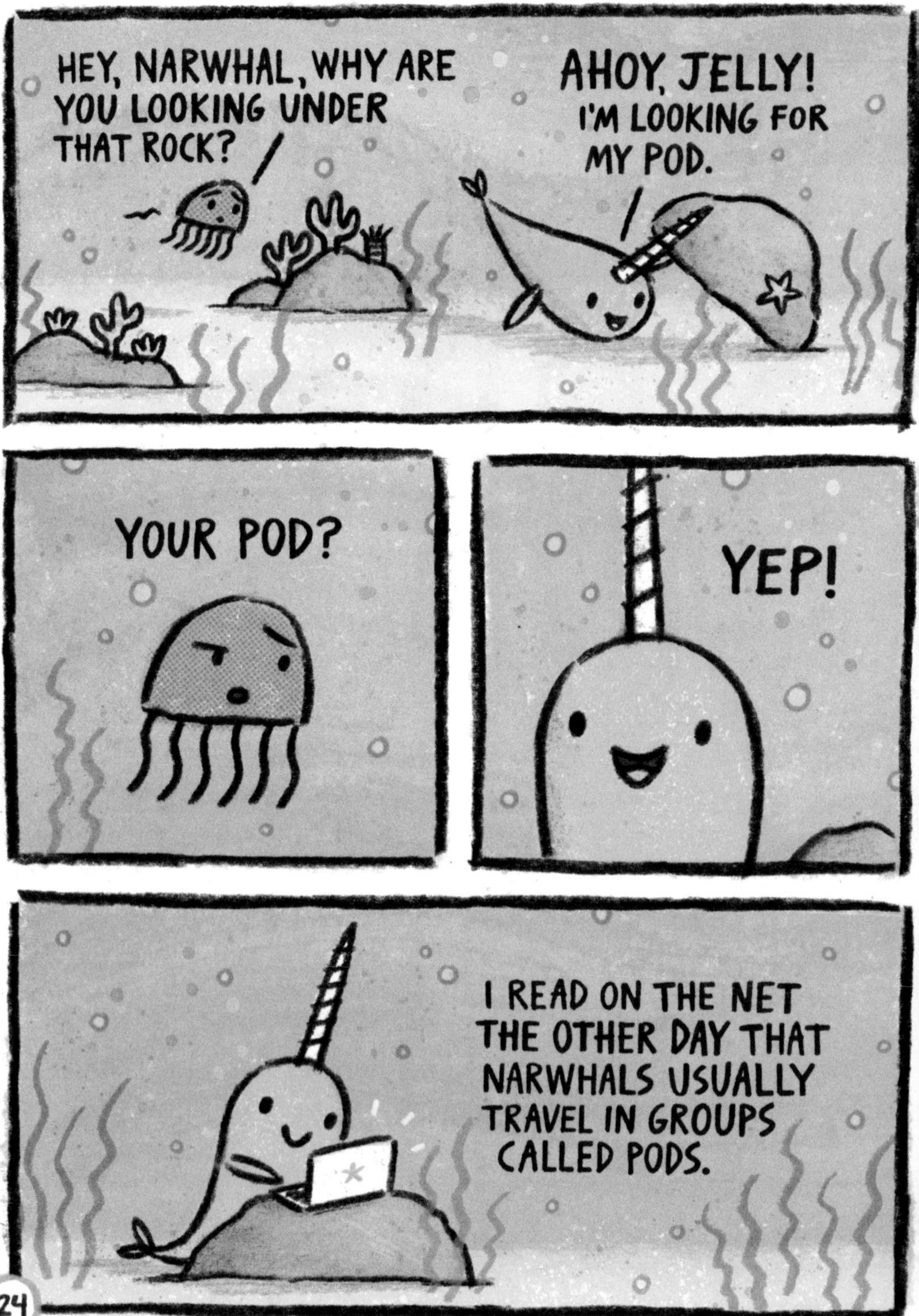
HEY, NARWHAL, WHY ARE YOU LOOKING UNDER THAT ROCK?
AHOY, JELLY!
I'M LOOKING FOR MY POD.
YOUR POD?
YEP!
I READ ON THE NET THE OTHER DAY THAT NARWHALS USUALLY TRAVEL IN GROUPS CALLED PODS.

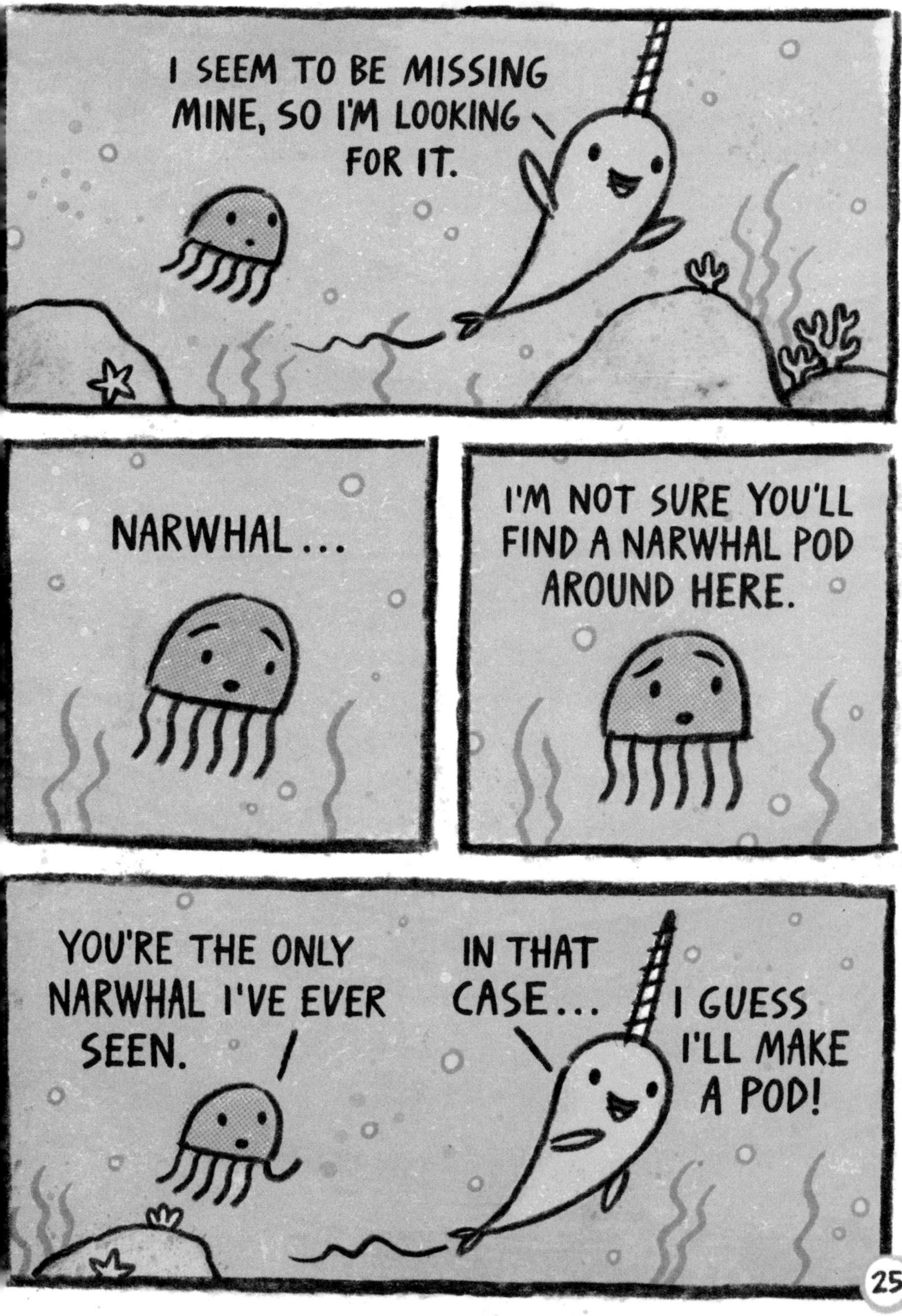

I SEEM TO BE MISSING MINE, SO I'M LOOKING FOR IT.
NARWHAL...
I'M NOT SURE YOU'LL FIND A NARWHAL POD AROUND HERE.
YOU'RE THE ONLY NARWHAL I'VE EVER SEEN.
IN THAT CASE...
I GUESS I'LL MAKE A POD!

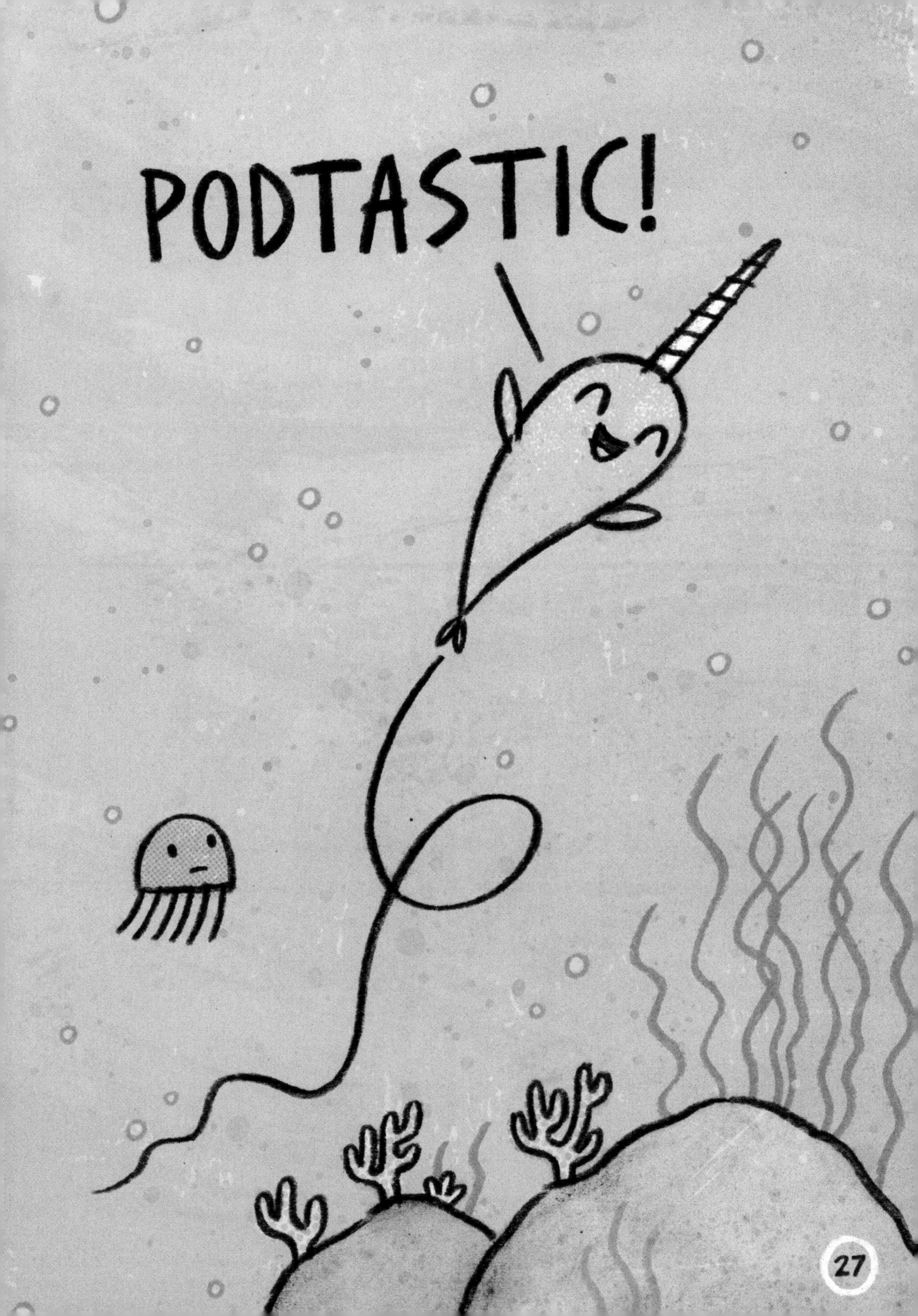
PODTASTIC!

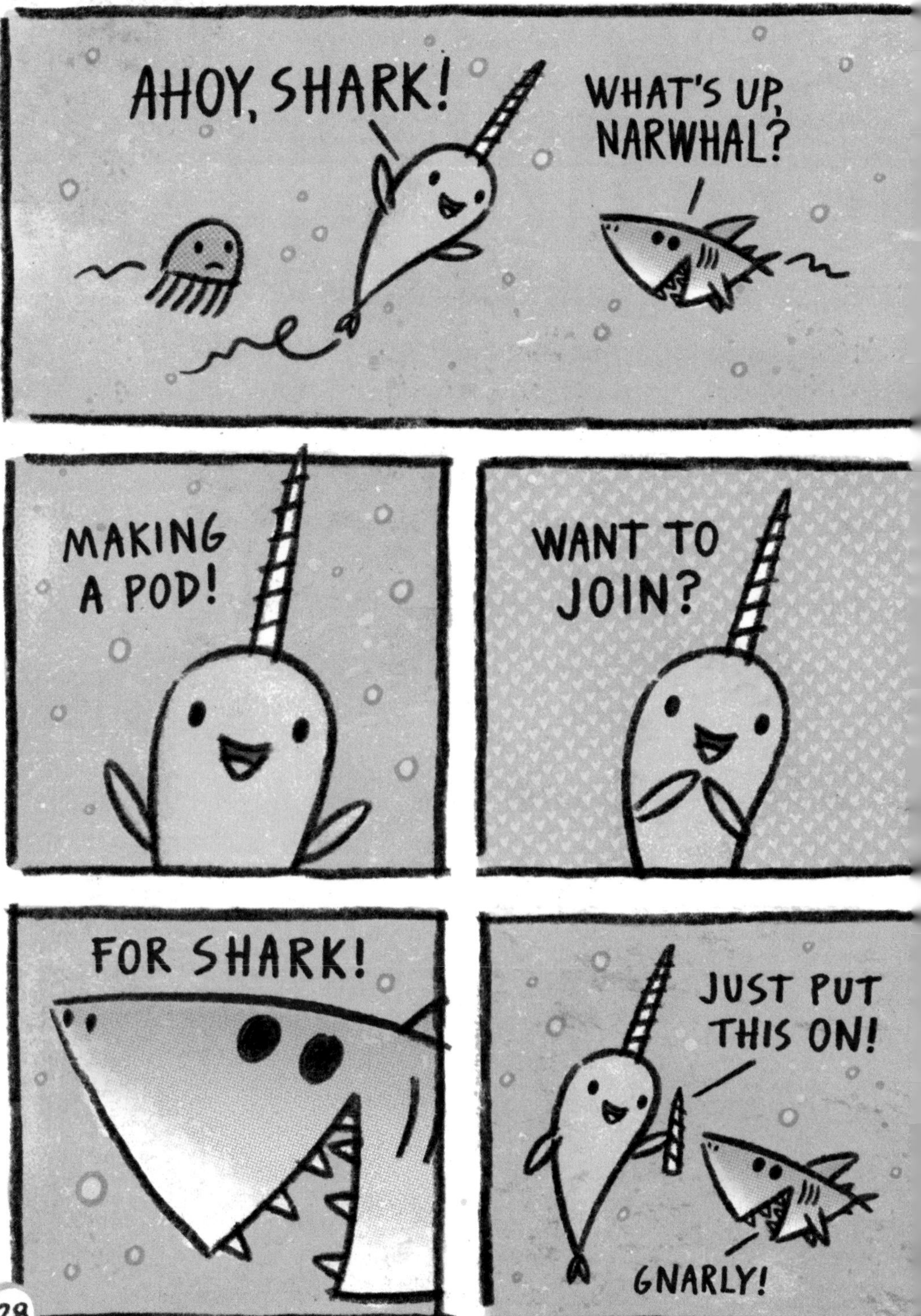
AHOY, SHARK!
WHAT'S UP, NARWHAL?
MAKING A POD!
WANT TO JOIN?
FOR SHARK!
JUST PUT THIS ON!
GNARLY!

29

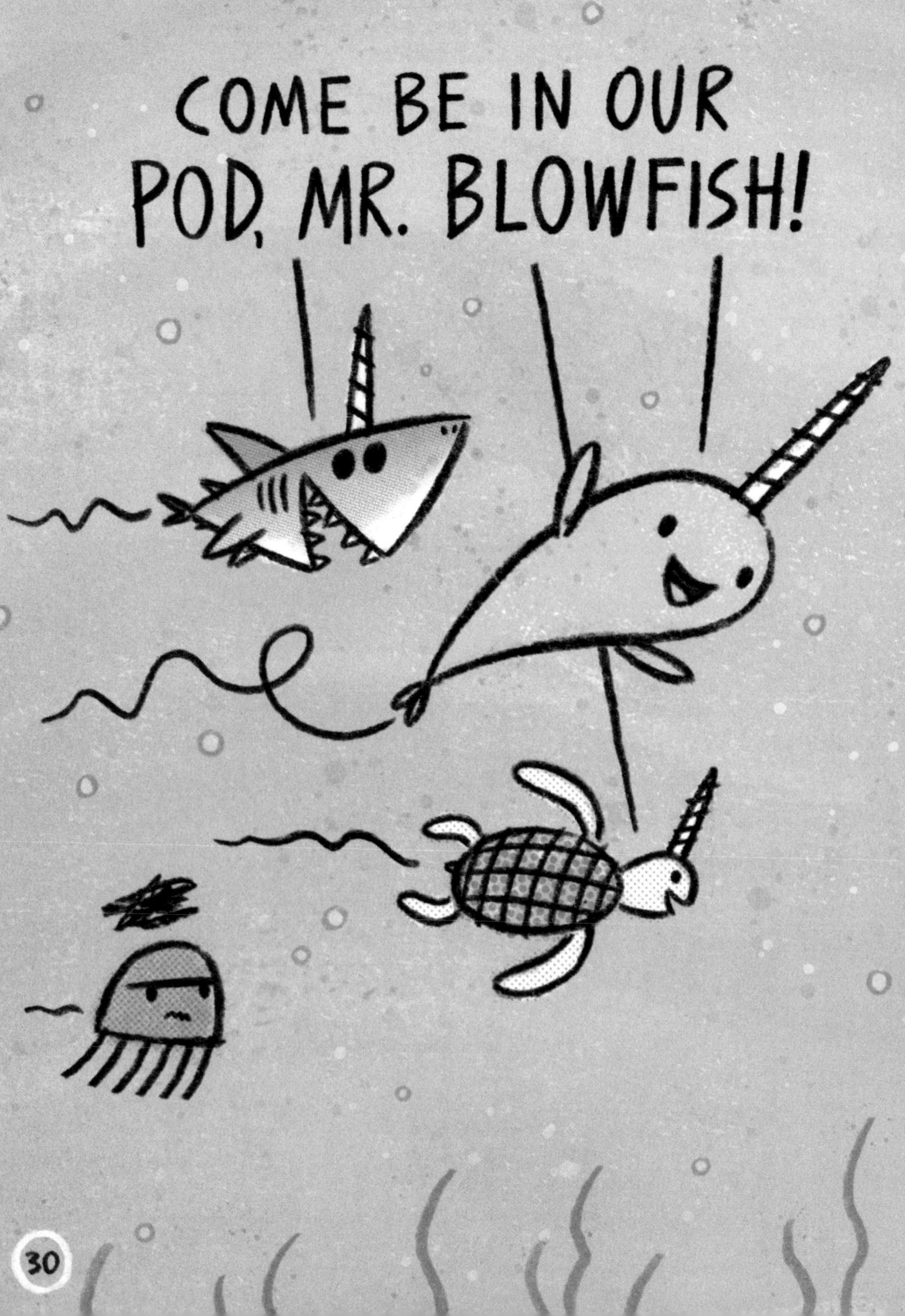
COME BE IN OUR POD, MR. BLOWFISH!

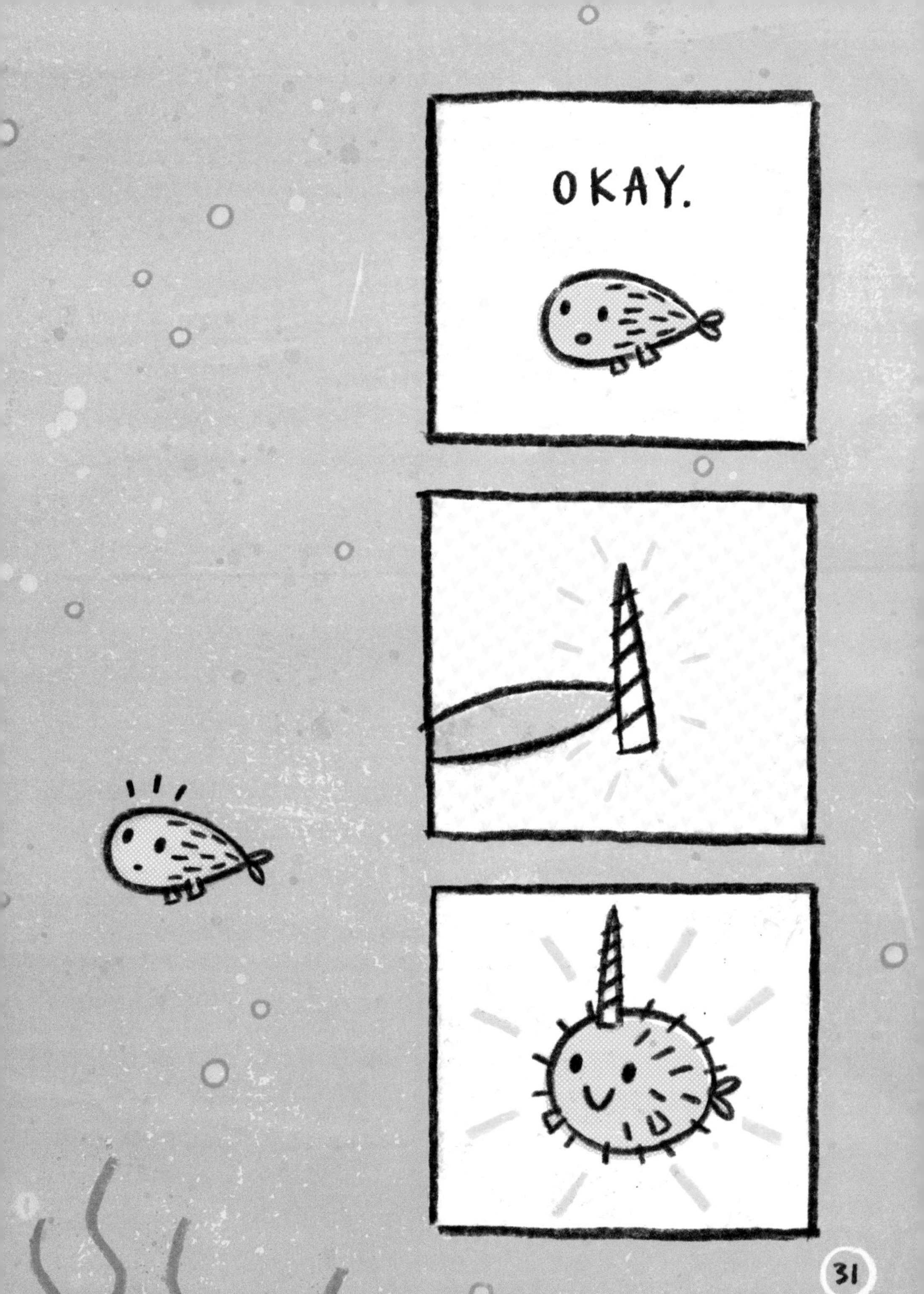
OKAY.

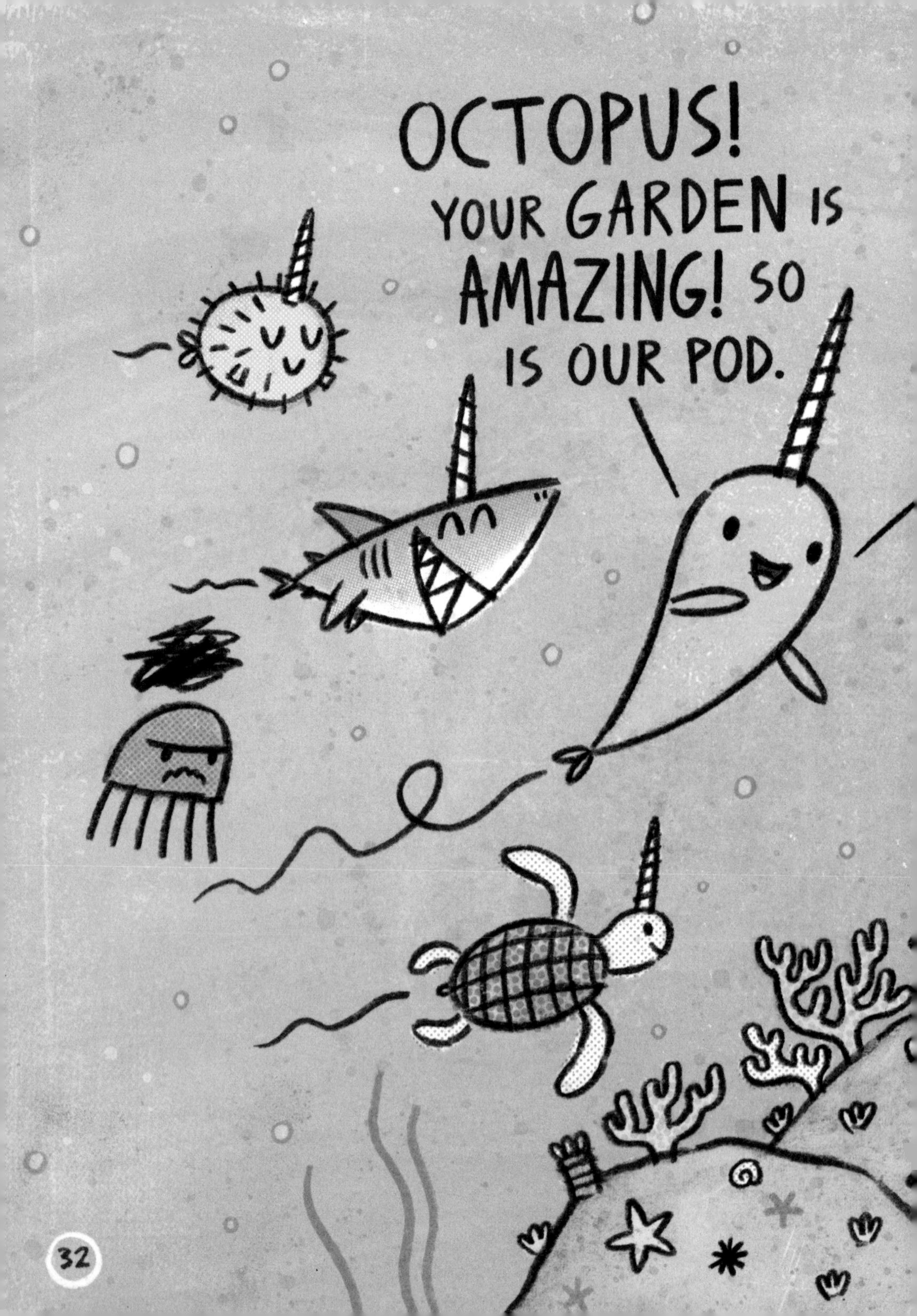
OCTOPUS! YOUR GARDEN IS AMAZING! SO IS OUR POD.

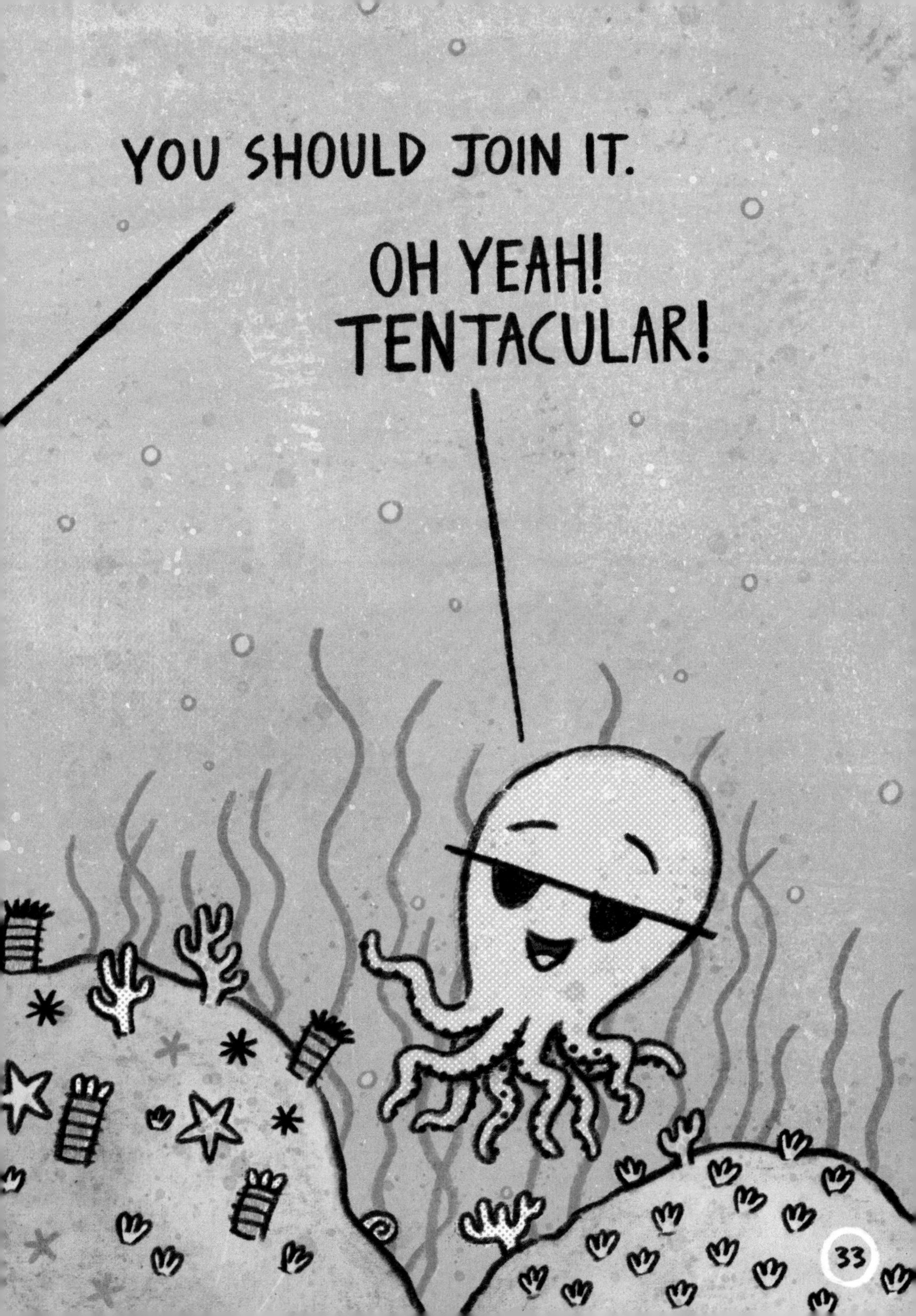
YOU SHOULD JOIN IT.
OH YEAH! TENTACULAR!

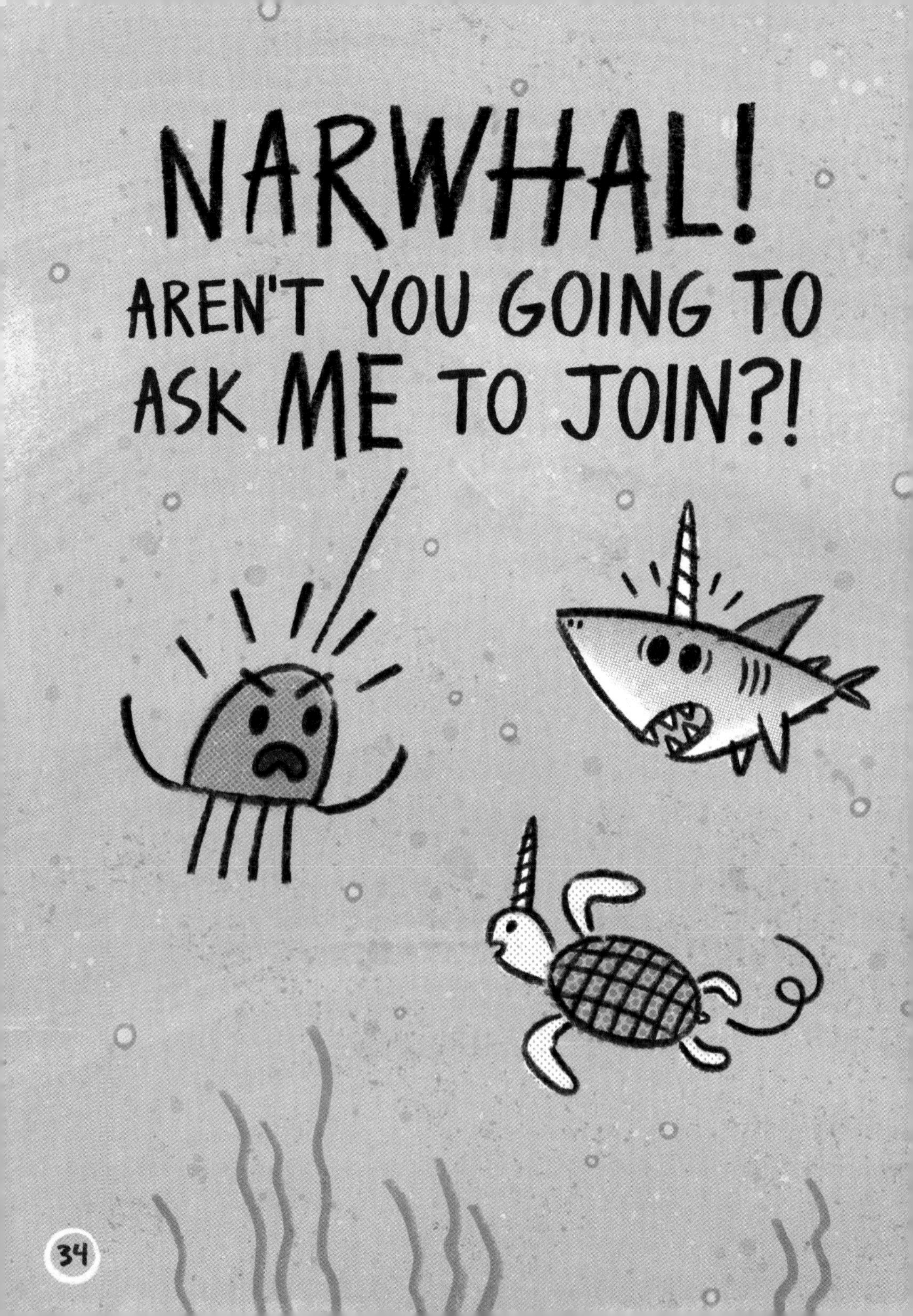
NARWHAL!
AREN'T YOU GOING TO ASK ME TO JOIN?!

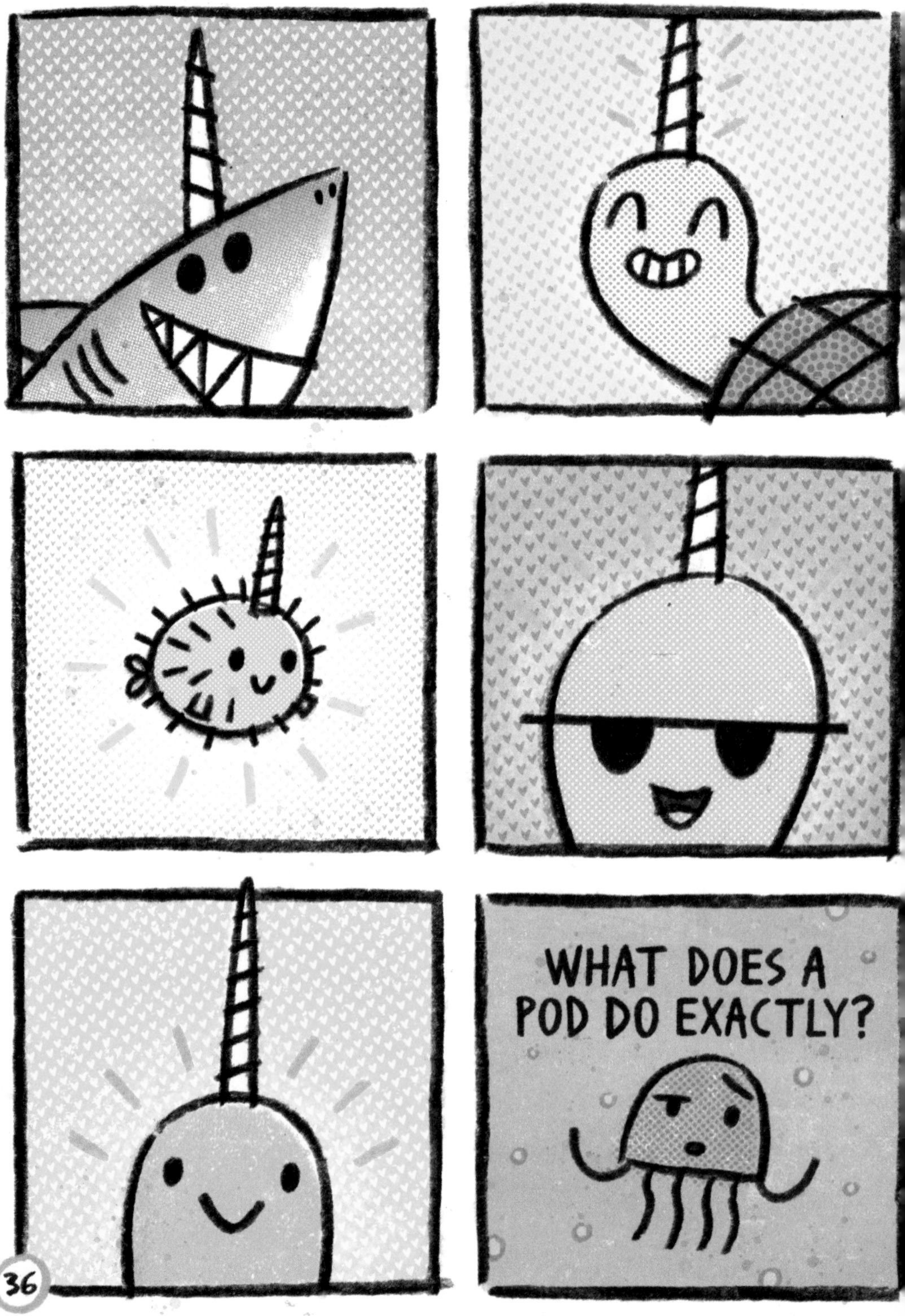
WHAT DOES A POD DO EXACTLY?

I'M NOT REALLY SURE!

BUT I IMAGINE A POD PLAYS
ULTIMATE CANNONBALL, EATS
WAFFLES, FIGHTS CRIME AND...

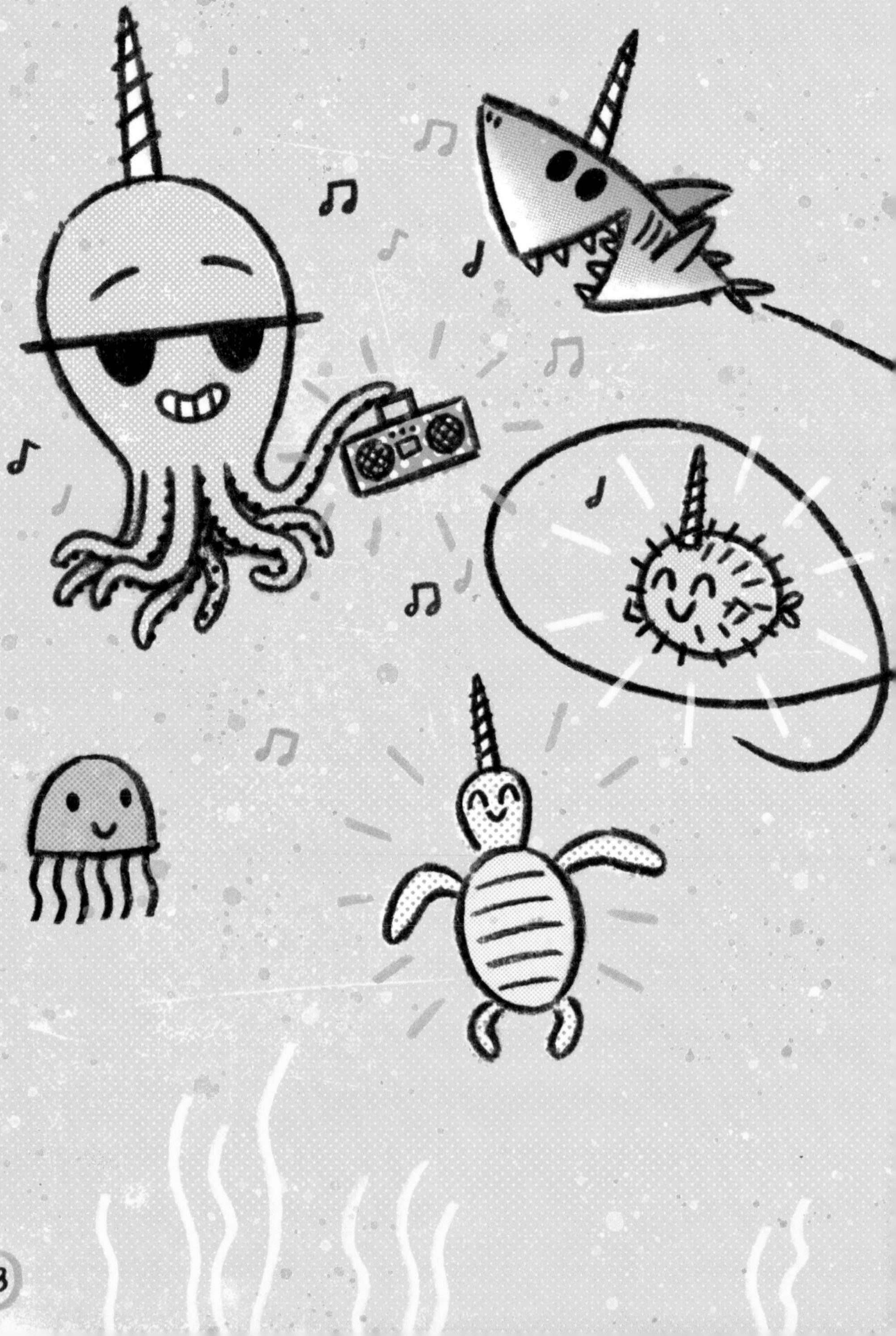

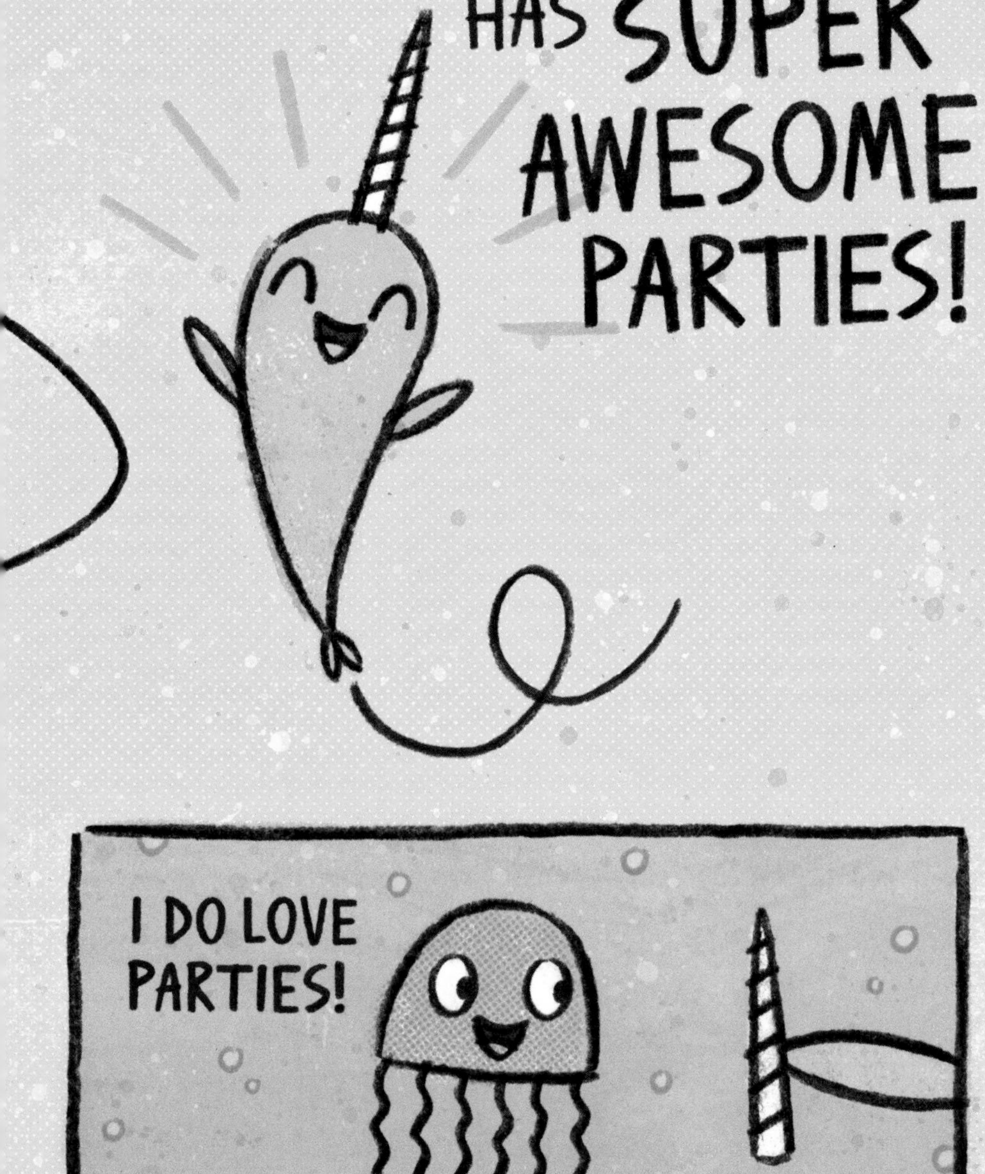
HAS SUPER AWESOME PARTIES!
I DO LOVE PARTIES!

PODTASTIC!

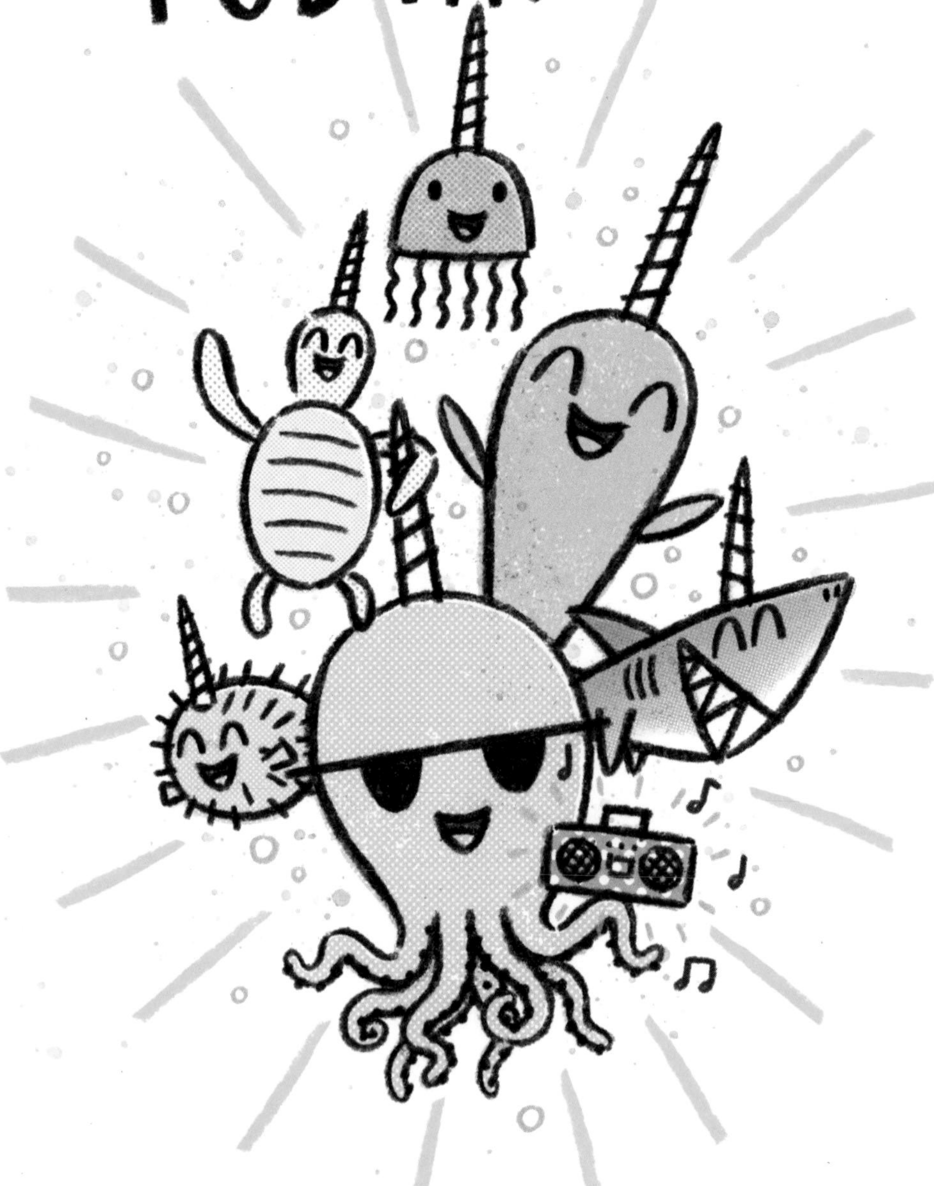

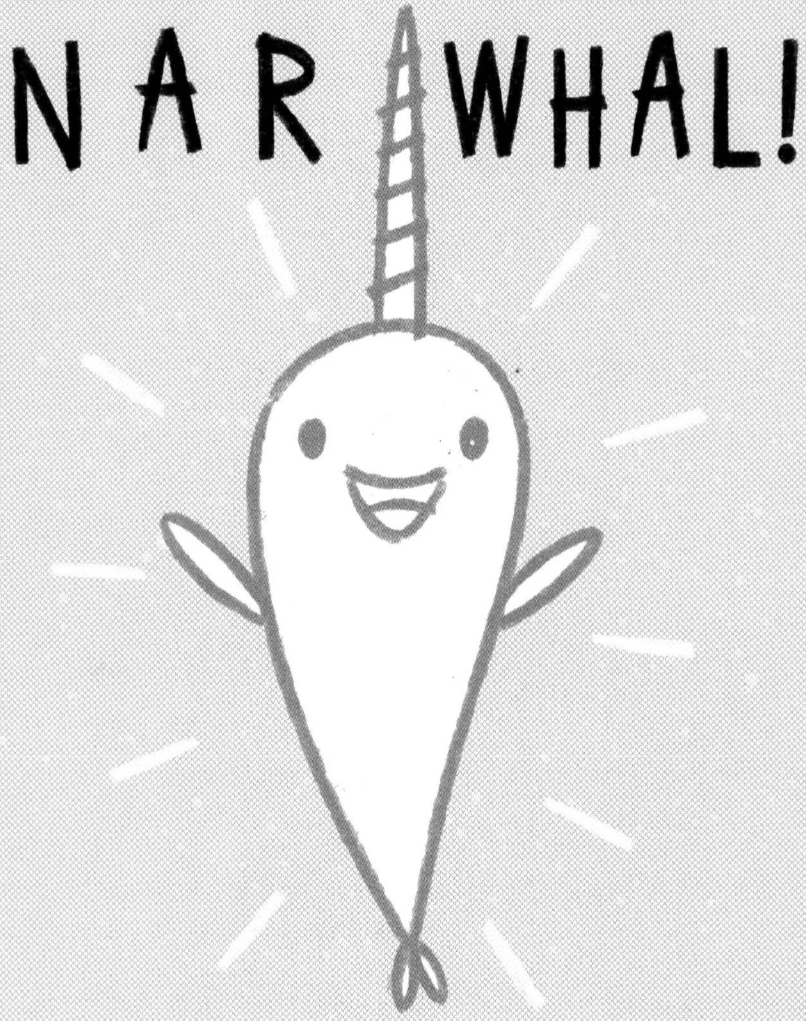
NARWHAL!

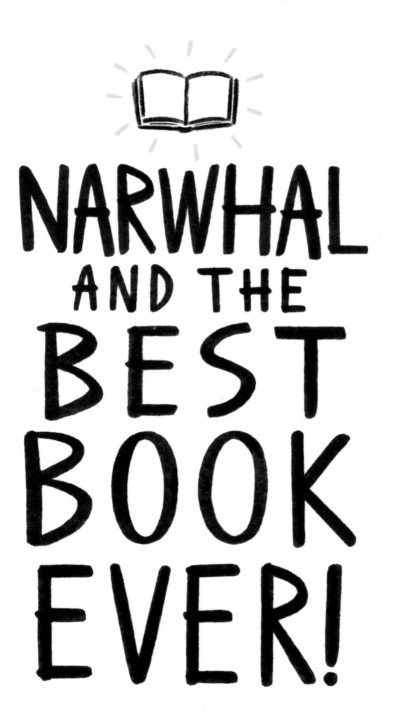

NARWHAL
AND THE
BEST
BOOK
EVER!

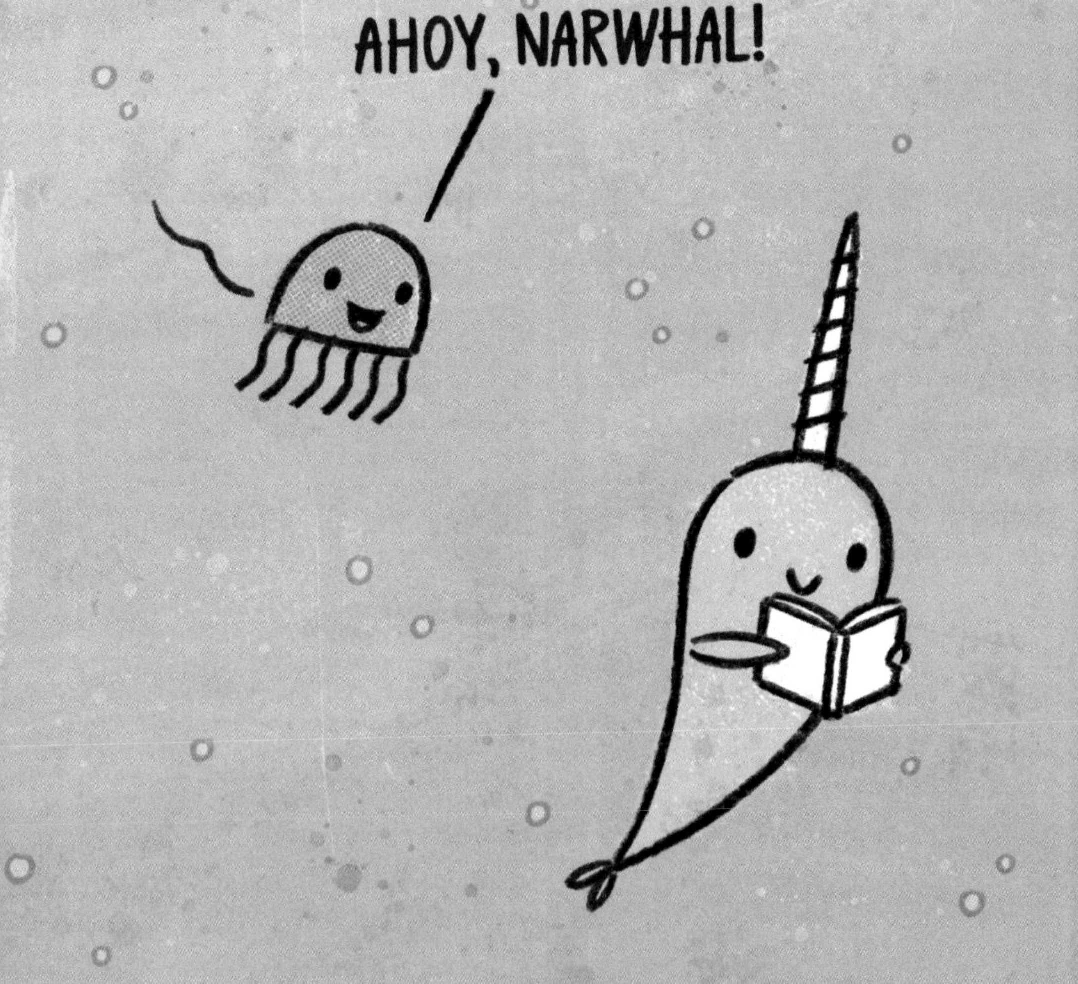
AHOY, NARWHAL!

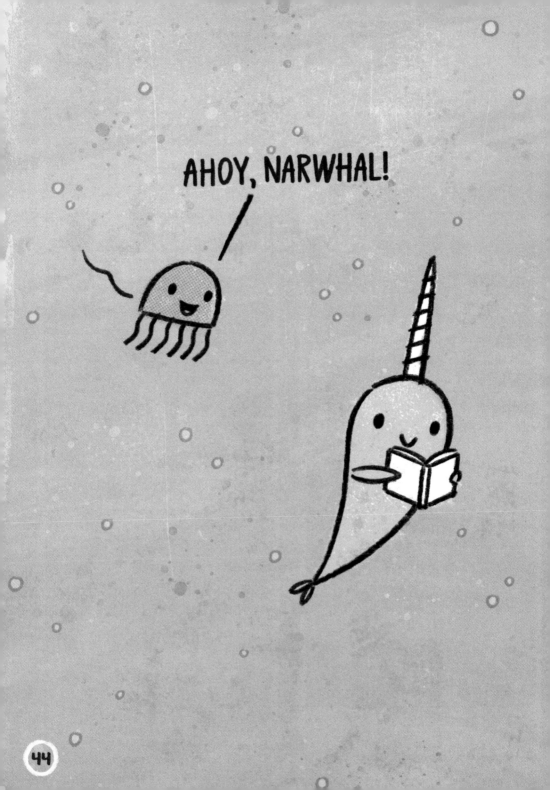

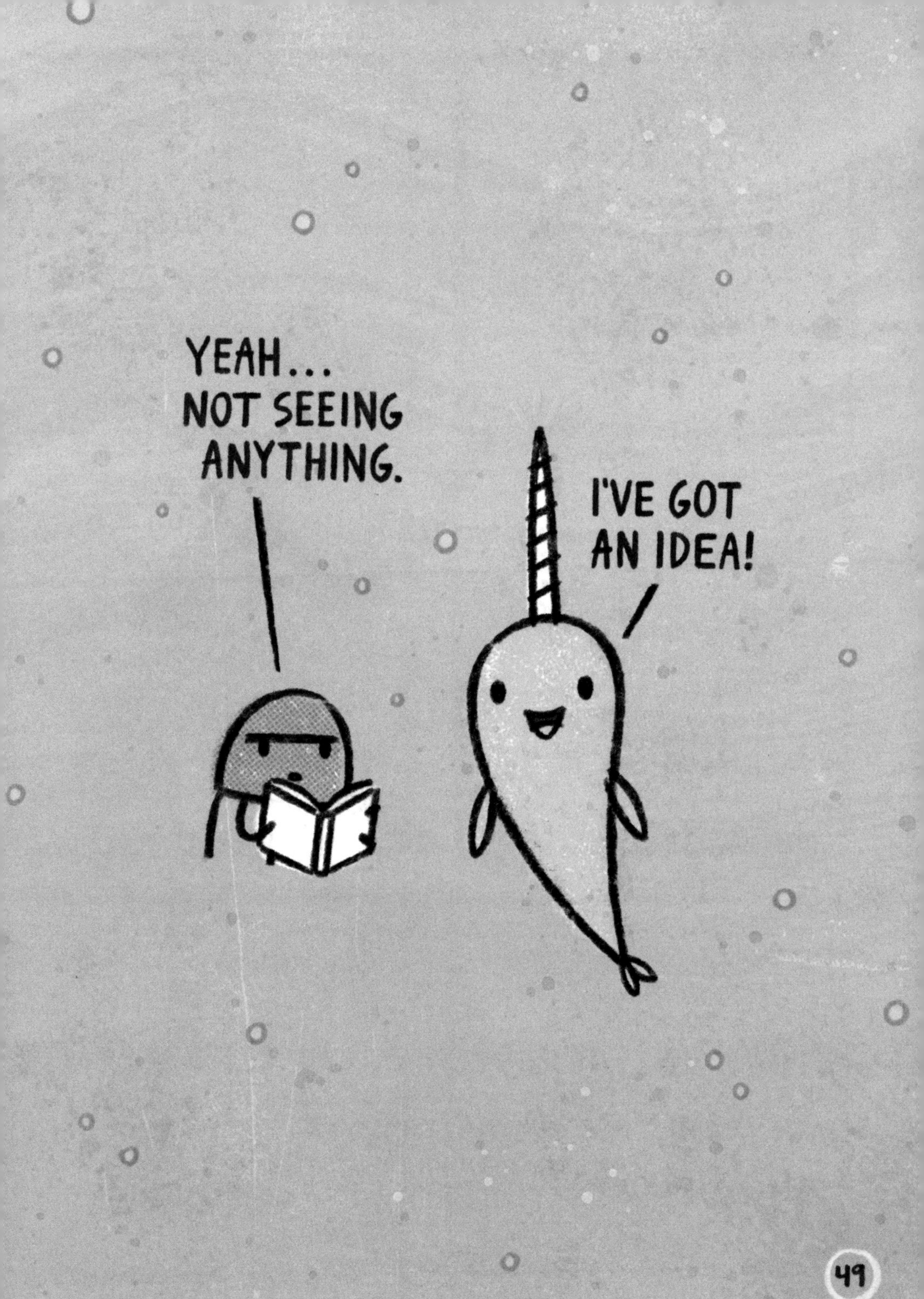
YEAH... NOT SEEING ANYTHING.
I'VE GOT AN IDEA!

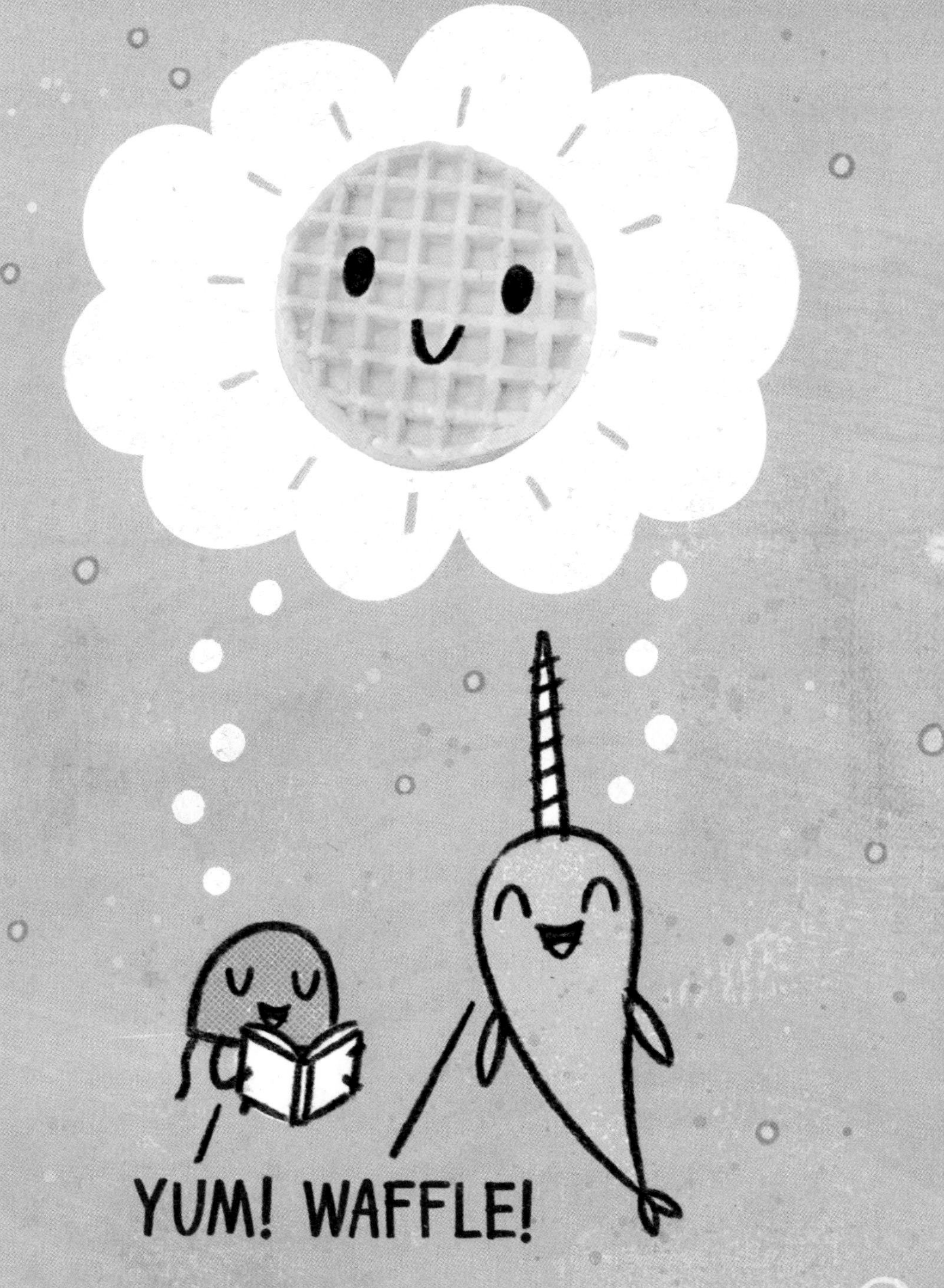
YUM! WAFFLE!

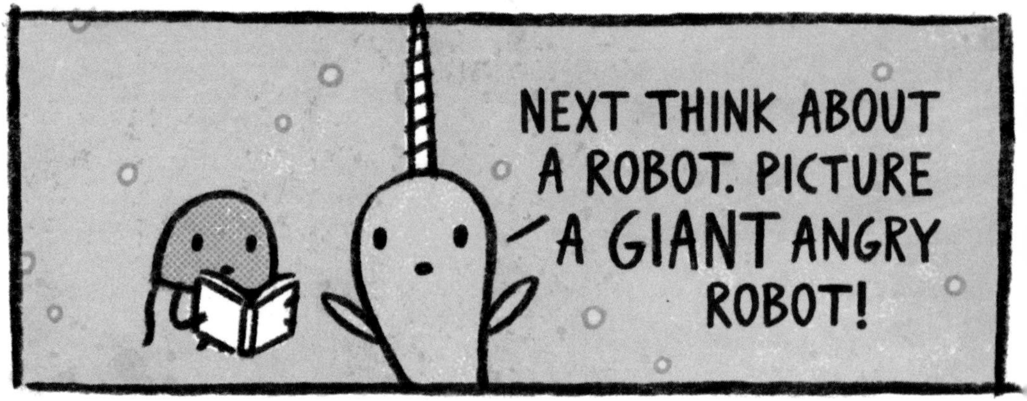
NEXT THINK ABOUT A ROBOT. PICTURE A GIANT ANGRY ROBOT!

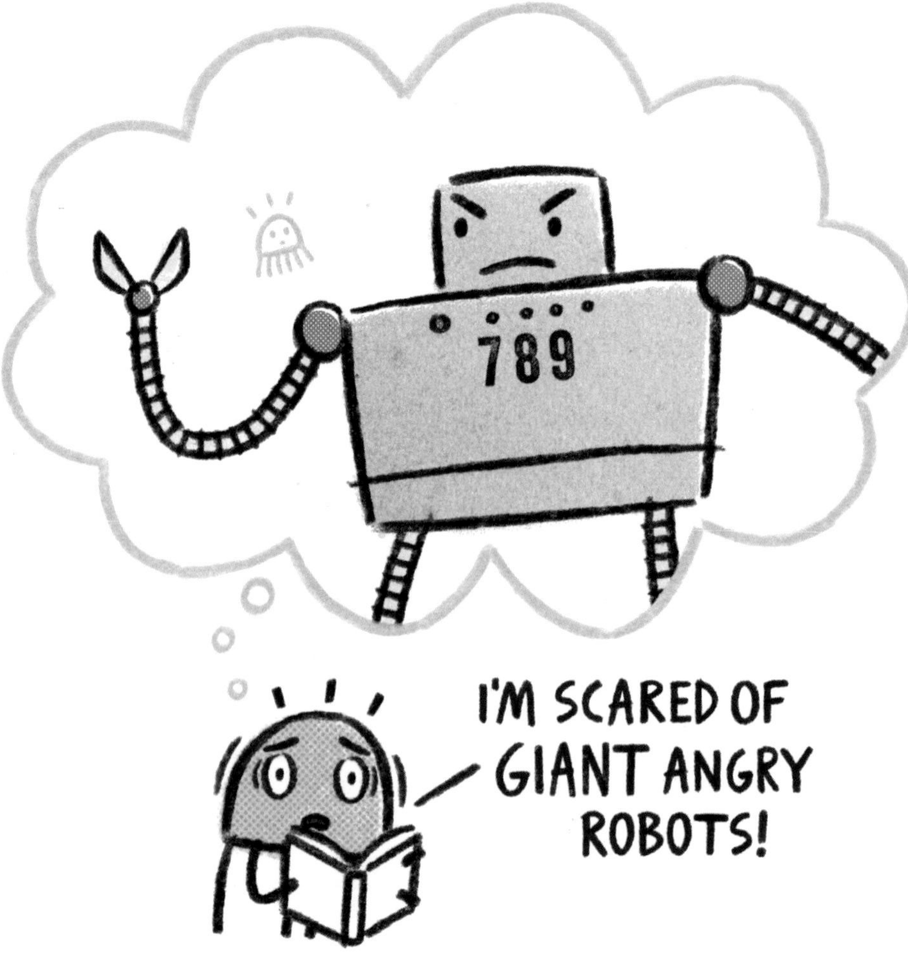
789
I'M SCARED OF GIANT ANGRY ROBOTS!

GOOD THING THAT WAFFLE
IS A KUNG FU MASTER!

LOOK AT THE BOOK AND SEE
A PICTURE OF IT BATTLING
THE ROBOT!

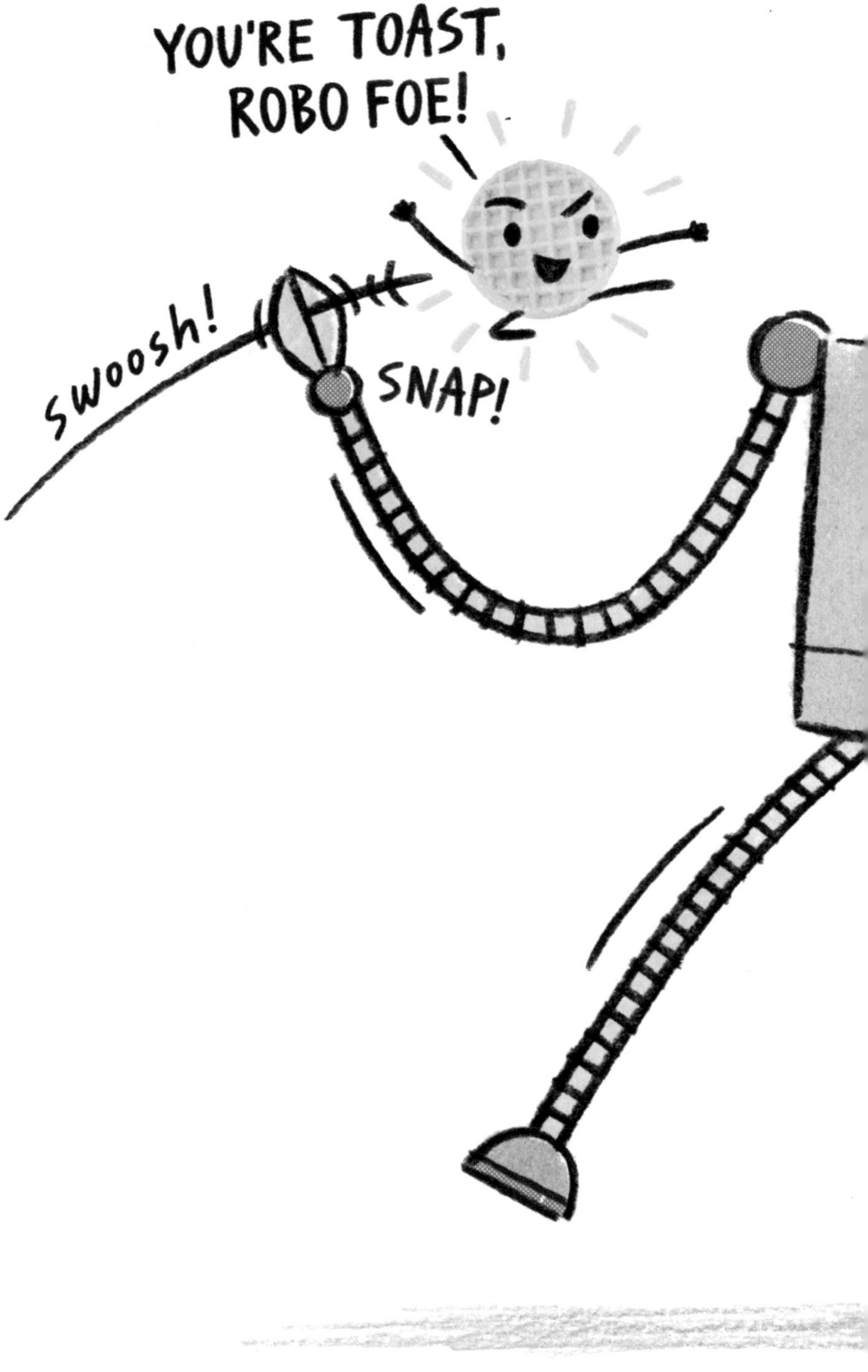
YOU'RE TOAST, ROBO FOE!
swoosh!
SNAP!

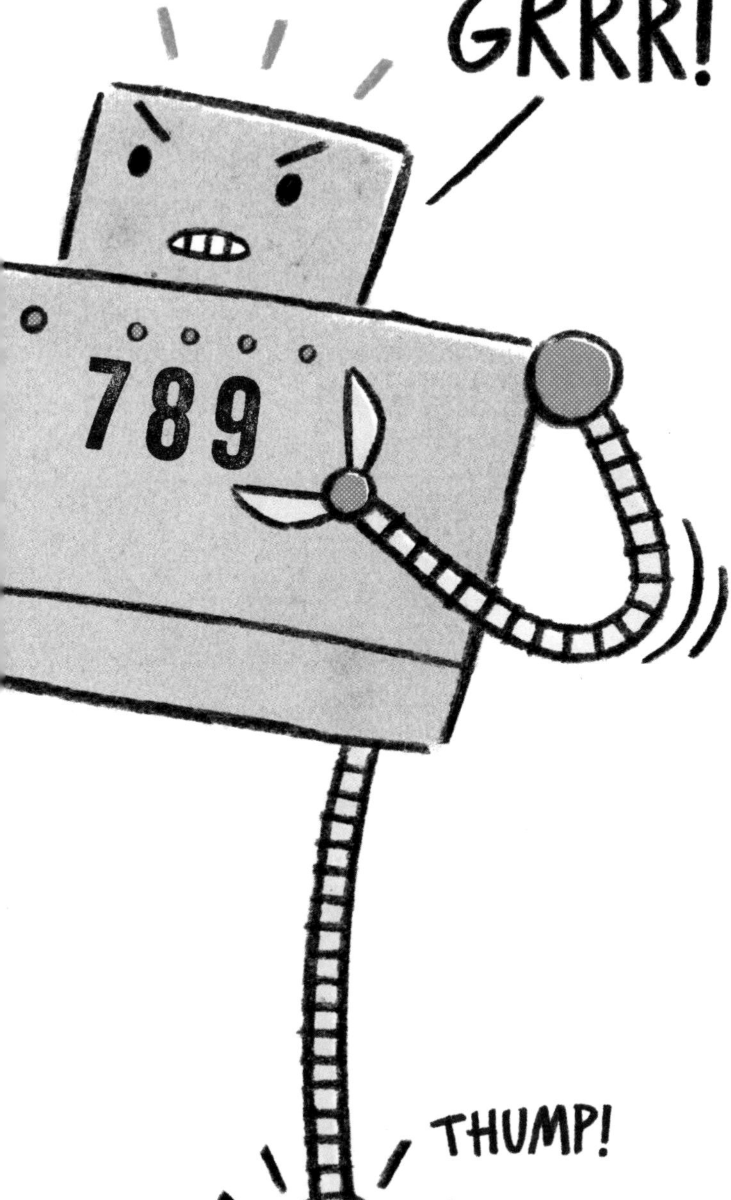
GRRR!
789
THUMP!

NICE ONE, JELLY!

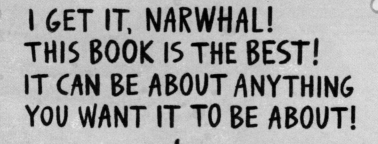

I GET IT, NARWHAL!
THIS BOOK IS THE BEST!
IT CAN BE ABOUT ANYTHING
YOU WANT IT TO BE ABOUT!

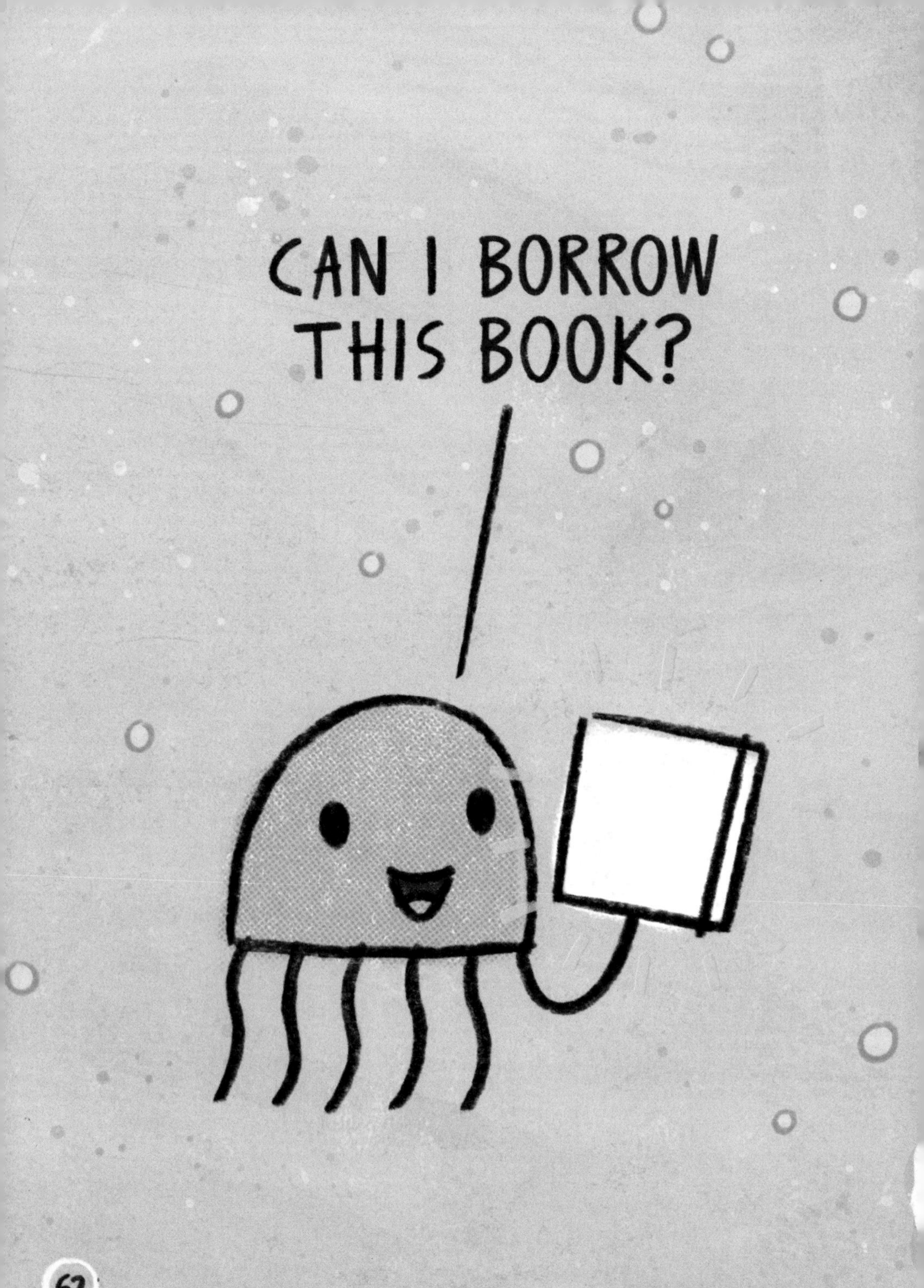
CAN I BORROW THIS BOOK?

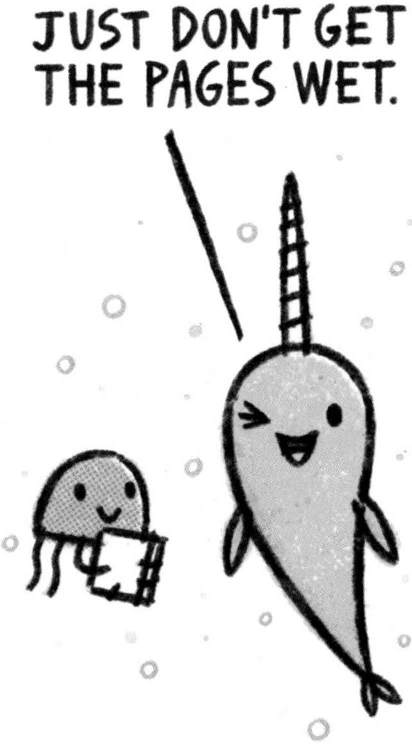
JUST DON'T GET
THE PAGES WET.

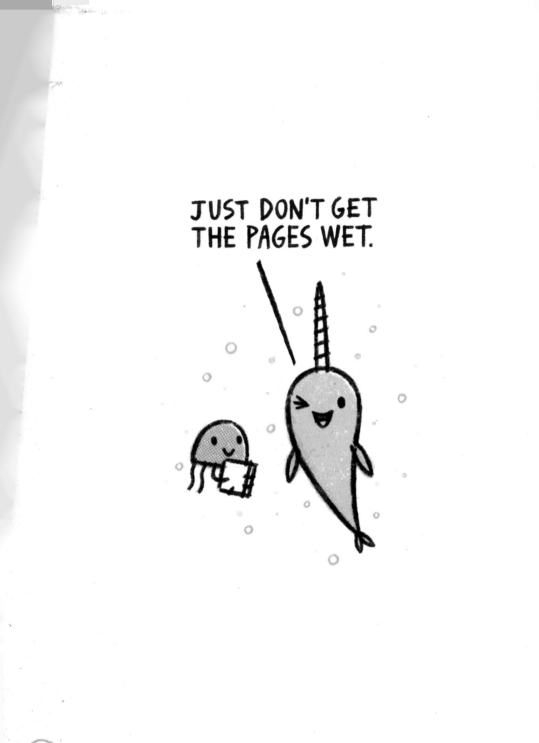

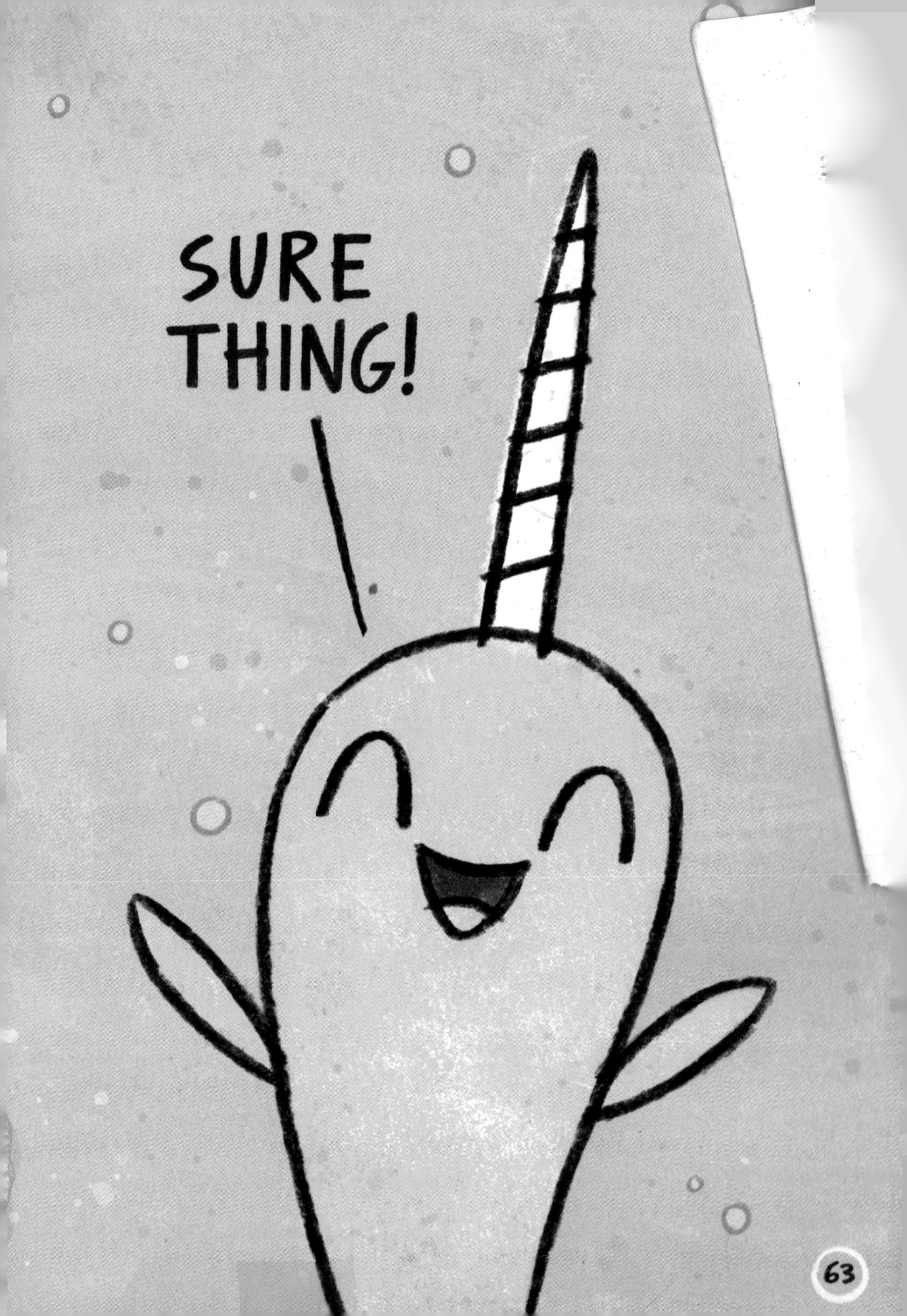
SURE THING!